BROKEN FLOWERS

Howard A Finkelstein

ISBN: 0692480927
ISBN 13: 9780692480922
Library of Congress Control Number: 2015945374
Howard Finkelstein, Los Angeles, CA

ACKNOWLEDGEMENTS

In memory of my loving mother, and father, who left too soon. And a special thanks to my beautiful wife Evguenia (Greta), who has never used an illegal drug in her life. She trusted an old, broken down ex drug addict, loved me, and gave me a reason to be a better man.

Cover photo by Alyssa Finkelstein of Hirhurim Photography.

AN AUTHOR'S NOTE

The people that I write about are all fictional. But I knew them all.

A moment of truth.

I became a drug addict when I was forty –two. Up until that time I was a very successful dog trainer, song writer, and businessman. I tried cocaine a few times and was hooked. In the eight years that followed, I smoked cocaine day and night. I became helplessly addicted, as I went through three quarters of a million dollars. I became a pusher, and a smuggler. I lost touch with my children, and everyone who was decent in my life.

The final three years of my existence I became homeless in New York City.

Living on the streets I grew to know the many dregs of humanity. I was one of them, and I was an observer. The day I turned fifty I stopped.

There are many more stories to tell, but these tragic lives will have to do for now.

"Broken Flowers" comes from my heart. Parents be aware of what your children are doing, and never give up on them. Those of you who think you just want to experiment, beware. The experiment just might blow up in your face. And for those of you who are hooked, stop. Reach out for any help you can find, and fight the drug. You CAN get your life back.

Howard Finkelstein
August 20, 2015

CHAPTER ONE

I t was a beautiful Tudor home nestled in a gated community in Beverly Hills.

The trappings of wealth were evident in one room after another. Several fine paintings hung in the entrance hall.

The downstairs rooms showed the touch of an expensive decorator with magnificent Persian rugs, crystal chandeliers, and original works of art. It was the maid's day off, but every surface was polished and perfect.

A carpeted stairway led to the second floor bedrooms and bathrooms. You could barely hear the muffled sounds of three people talking behind one mahogany door. Two of the voices coming from behind the mahogany door were young men, and one was a young woman.

Valarie put down the glass pipe she was holding as she whispered, "Whew! My head was spinning for a second there."

Her brother Jeffrey, replied, "Spinning is good, Valarie. You want your head to spin."

Their friend Stu announced that he was thirsty, and he went to get some ice water.

This was the home of Karen Campel, a beautiful successful television soap opera star who had worked hard as a single parent to raise her son and her daughter. She was proud of the secure life she had provided for them.

CHAPTER TWO

Jeffery and Valarie Campel, along with their best friend Stuart Bean, were doing an oft repeated afternoon activity. Jeffrey's room contained his bed and dresser, a chair, a desk, and a lamp. The room was decorated like a privileged young man's room might be. There were framed pictures of girlfriends, of certain athletes, and a picture of a clean cut younger Jeffery, graduating from Beverly Hills High School.

Now, two years after graduating, both he and Stu looked like rebellious long-haired rich kids.

"Just growing pains," their mothers would say.

Valarie was a lovely fifteen-year-old girl, who idolized her older brother.

As Stu came back from his ice water break Valarie asked Jeffery what time their mother was expected home.

Jeffery checked his watch and answered, "Don't sweat it. We have plenty of time."

On the desk were all the supplies they needed to continue their freebasing party. There was a glass bottom tray, ten vials of crack, a torch, two glass pipes, and a lighter. Valarie put half of the contents of a vile of crack cocaine in one of the pipes. She handed the pipe to Stu.

"It's your turn Stuie."

Stu told Jeffery, "You're lucky you have such a cool kid sister. Now I know why you like to get high with her. She's better than my old lady."

Then Stu lit the torch, heated the pipe and did the hit.

"Hey Stu, Valarie's been a 'head' for over two years already. Listen, Mom might be here soon, so we have to finish and burn some incense."

Valarie reached over, picked up a pipe, and poured an entire vial into it. She then added a second vial to the first. Before she started to heat the pipe she said to Stu, "That always fools Mom." Then mimicking her mother she said, "I hate the smell of that incense you kids burn so often."

They all shared a laugh inspired by Valarie's imitation, and their own sense of "getting over." Stu proclaimed, "Wow, that's going to be a super blast."

Valarie happily added, "You guys just watch Jeffery's baby sister do her thing."

Valarie lit the torch and heated the pipe, and then started to inhale the smoke. She continued and continued until she completely filled her lungs. It was a long gigantic hit. Then Valarie handed the pipe and torch to Stu, who turned off the torch and put them down. The boys were watching Valarie, and were tripping out on the hit she had taken. Valarie held her breath for as long as she could. When she could not hold back anymore, she let the smoke out in a huge exhale. Jeff's voice was filled with admiration as he told her, "That was one hell of a blast."

Suddenly, Valarie's eyes went wide, and her body went absolutely stiff. A horrible sound was coming from her throat, like a constricted scream as she fell backwards. Even though this was happening in front of the two men, her fall was like she was thrown backward. They could not catch her, and she hit the floor hard.

Jeff dropped to one knee beside her as he was starting to panic. "My God, Stu she's overdosed. What do we do?"

Stu was on the floor next to Jeff. "Don't panic man, don't panic."

Jeff grabbed Valarie's shoulders and shook her. Valarie's legs were convulsing. There was drool coming from her mouth.

Stu was screaming in her ear. "Valarie, Valarie! Do you hear me; do you hear me dam it? Stu, go get some ice water. A lot of it. Hurry man!"

As Jeff ran out the door Stu continued to shake the girl. Her legs stopped shaking and her eyes were starting to close.

"Hurry, Jeff we're losing her."

Stu slapped Valarie sharply across the face. There was a slight reaction. Her legs started to twitch as Jeff came running into the room with two buckets of ice water.

"Quick, throw a bucket on her face." Jeffery did so. The water drenched Valarie's hair and shoulders. Her legs started to convulse again.

Jeffery was crying, "Valarie don't die. Please don't die."

"Quick, throw the other bucket on her face."

Jeff was crying and became more useless.

Stu snapped at Jeffery," Do it Jeffery. Fuck man, do it now."

That helped mobilize Jeff. He threw the second bucket of water in his sister's face. Her whole body went into convulsions.

"Jeff, help me get her up. Help me stand her up."

Valarie's body was not totally stiff, but she was still out and dead weight as the two boys picked her up by her underarms.

"We've got to make her walk. Come on Valarie, walk"

Jeff started to beg her "Come on Val, walk, walk, walk. Please Val, walk."

As the boys dragged her across the floor, Valarie's body started to stiffen again. Then she suffered another convulsion. Stu lost his grip on her, and she fell onto the bed. Valarie's body was stiff again.

"Oh, God, Stu, we're losing her. We're losing her."

Jeff felt totally helpless, as he cried uncontrollably.

"Jeff, help me get her into the bathroom."

"What are we going to try there, Stu?"

"Just do it."

Stu grabbed Valarie under her arms, as Jeff tried to take her feet. The stiffening of her body, her convulsions, and her dead weight made it impossible to carry her. Instead, together they half dragged and, half carried her to the nearest bathroom. As they started to pull her through the door, Stu took over the task of dragging her himself.

"We've got to try one more thing, Jeff. Get me some ice cubes."

Jeff was going into shock, and didn't move. Stu yelled, "Jeff, get me some ice cubes, and hurry up."

Jeff was mobilized and bolted out the door. Stu was busy pulling off Valarie's soaked pajama bottoms, and putting her in the bathtub.

Jeff ran into the room with a bucket of ice cubes.

Jeff saw Valarie in the bathtub. The shower was soaking her with cold water. Her pajama bottoms and panties were lying in a wad by the edge of the bed. Stu was also in the shower.

"Give me the ice cubes," Stu said as he grabbed a handfull. Stu then put the cubes between Valarie's legs, and into her vagina.

"The shock sometimes brings them out of it."

Valarie started to shake, and her eyes cracked open. She was not out of it yet, but she was coming back. She asked, "Is it my turn?"

Jeff and Valarie's mother appeared in the doorway. She looked lovely as she screamed in terror, and fainted.

"

CHAPTER THREE

D r. Mary Crawford was walking down the hallway of her very
expensive Century City office building. She was fifty years
old, but she could pass for thirty-eight. She was a beautiful woman.
The conservative business suit she was wearing did not hide her
full breasts. As she walked past several offices doors of high priced
lawyers and stock brokers, her strong well-shaped legs moved with
confidence. When she reached her office, she felt that usual wave
of pleasure, as she read the sign on the door: Dr. Mary Crawford
M.D. Psychotherapist – Psycho Hypnosis.

Dr. Crawford walked into her office and made sure everything
was in order.

There was a large modern desk, and a reception desk. There
were matched designer chairs, and a small couch for clients. On
the walls were pictures of Dr. Crawford with well known politi-
cians and actors. There were also framed diplomas from Harvard
Medical School, and various graduate schools of psychiatry and
Hypnotherapy. In a corner of the room, a small antique desk displayed five books that were authored by Dr. Crawford. Two of the

books were on the subject of hypnosis, two on psychiatry, and one on suicide prevention. On a wall, there was prominently displayed a plaque from her publisher, for the suicide prevention book reaching best-seller status.

Satisfied that all was in place, Dr. Crawford said hello to her Secretary Sharon, who returned the greeting.

Sharon was a thirty-year-old woman, plain in appearance, and strictly businesslike. Dr. Crawford walked to her own desk, and picked up the mail that Sharon had placed on it. That this was done with a familiarity that indicated this was routine. Then Sharon relayed the telephone messages.

"The hospital called, and reported that the Johnson boy and the Phillips girl had no irregularities through the night. Your one o'clock appointment with Edward Styles cancelled. He will call to reschedule. The rest of the day is set, unless an emergency comes up. All six members of the group encounter meeting are inside waiting for you. They were all on time today."

As Sharon was going over the last details, Dr. Crawford was looking out of her window, at the canopied entrance to her building. There was a bank of pay telephones to the right of the entrance. She noticed a shaggy young man talking on a pay telephone. Perhaps it was her imagination, but he seemed to be looking up at her

"Sharon, I've seen that man by that phone for several days now. I'm quite sure that he's doing drug deals. Write another letter to the chief of police. Copy it to Mayor Garcetti, and to the telephone company. Write it on my personal stationary. If the police won't do anything about it, perhaps we can get the telephone company to remove the phones.

Next, Dr Crawford went into her personal office. It was richly adorned with an antique roll top desk and chair, a Louis the XIV settee, and a small file cabinet. The walls were a rich mahogany, but were devoid of any pictures. The one window looked out at the same scene as the front office window.

Then, Dr. Crawford went through another door, and entered the therapy room.

The therapy room was six- hundred- square- feet. It was void of all the rich appointments of the rest of the office. At this time, there were six hard, wooden chairs, arranged in a slight semi-circle. The chairs were purposely uncomfortable.

Positioned four feet from the chairs and facing them, was a white cushioned chair. It was higher than the other chairs, to immediately establish control. The chair had several buttons and lights built into the armrests, as well as a telephone port. The buttons could be used to alter the temperature in the room, and raise or dim the lights. There was a buzzer and a light, for the intercom with Sharon. And the chair could swivel, so that Dr. Crawford could directly face each patient.

The members of the group included Andrew, a sixteen-year-old white boy from Encino. He was thin and frail, and he had an angry, boisterous attitude.

Peggy was fifteen. She was fat and unattractive, withdrawn, and introverted.

Valarie was now sixteen. She was dark haired, and blossoming into a very beautiful young woman.

Her brother Jeffery was barely eighteen. He now had short hair, and he was soon to enter the Navy.

Peter was sixteen, and very intelligent. He was also of medium build and rather average in appearance.

The sixth member of the group was David. David was nineteen, and was tall and lean. He had a smoldering appearance, long hair and sensitive hands.

They were seated with the empty chair facing the center of the group.

David was in the first chair on the far left, then Peggy next to Andrew, Valarie was next, and then Peter, and Jeffrey.

There was good natured small talk going on in the group. They were all dressed casually, but dressed very expensively.

Dr. Crawford entered the room, and walked to a closet. The closet was positioned in a way that, when it was open, the group could not see its inside.

Dr. Crawford opened the door, reached into the closet, and took out a pack of cigarettes. Then, she closed the door and eased over to her seat. She barely brushed her hip against David as she passed him, and sat down.

The group turned their attention to Dr. Crawford. There was a friendly atmosphere in the room, as she was their leader and their friend.

They knew Dr. Crawford was there to help them, and the group thought of her as a hip mother, someone to love, and understand them.

Dr. Crawford started the meeting. "Good morning... Every day I hope that each of you is feeling a little better about yourself, and your recovery."

She paused as she received nods of assent.

"We've come a long way as a group, with exercises to help you control the urges you feel for your various addictions. I've also started to train you in how to redirect your negative desires. Now at this stage it is important to understand the reasons, and the consequences of your drug use. Over the weeks to come, I am going to open each of you up, and let the rest of us see you, and heal those wounds within you. It is my goal to send each one of you into the world, as whole, complete human beings. Do I have a volunteer? Who would like to go first?"

The group looked down and away from Dr. Crawford, and from each other. They were embarrassed and inhibited.

Dr. Crawford swiveled her chair so that she faced Peter directly. "I'm going to ask Peter to start. I will help you, Peter."

"I don't want to, Dr. Crawford. I'm not ready to. Please let."

Dr. Crawford interrupted him, "What was your drug of choice, Peter?"

"Amphetamines, please Dr. Crawford, I really don't want to talk right now,"

Andrew called out, "Come on Peter, you can do it."

Valarie asked, "Does he have to?"

Andrew tried to tease him, "Come on Peter, and be a man."

David joined in. "Peter, sooner or later we all have to do it."

Jeffery was unusually quiet.

Dr. Crawford interrupted, "That's enough! Andrew, be still! Valarie, sit up! And David, be quiet. You are all here with serious problems. It's my mission to solve your problems. Now nobody has to be here. Andrew you can go back to juvenile hall. Valarie and Jeffery you can face your mother, and explain to her that she has wasted a lot of money. Peter, I don't think you want to return to state prison, do you? And David, you were near dead when I found you! If you don't want my help."

Dr. Crawford paused, to let her words sink in. Then her tone changed.

"Do I sound hard? Rough?"

Various moans and responses came from the group.

"Listen, my young friends. If you've never heard the phrase tough love, now you have.

There is a reason why I'm paid very well for the work that I do. I am internationally known for my work in drug addiction, and suicide prevention. I will not permit any of you to cause me to fail! I will teach you to control your addictions, and I will cure you. Not one of you will ever even consider taking your own life! I will teach you how to live life one day at a time, while you plan your futures.

You may love me for it, or you may hate me for it. But you will learn how to take control of your lives."

CHAPTER FOUR

Dr. Crawford redirected her attention to Peter. "Please continue, Peter."

Peter thought for a second, before he started.

"I guess you could say that I was a little too smart for my own good. I went through primary school in an accelerated course, and was accepted to Poly Science High School. Only smart kids go there. During my first year, my friends and I set up a lab in my garage. My parents thought it was cool, that we spent our free time on school experiments. They didn't know we were making meth. We just wanted to see if we could make the stuff. And when we made it, we tried it." Peter paused, as it was difficult to continue.

Dr. Crawford reached down to a button on the right side of her chair. She held it down, and the lights began to dim.

"You're doing fine, Peter. Please continue."

Peter was reluctant to say more, but he blurted out the rest.

"There isn't much to tell. We got hooked on the stuff. Then we started making enough of the stuff to sell, so we could afford to do more ourselves. Something happened, and I got busted. Now I'm here in rehab."

Dr Crawford pressed the button again, bringing the room to near darkness. Then she took a pencil shaped flashlight from her pocket. She was now facing Peter.

"I'm going to place you in a hypnotic state now."

Dr. Crawford was in complete control. Her attitude and tone left no room for dissent.

She pointed the pencil flashlight upward, and turned it on, so that its muted pulsing beam fell directly on her face. The light made her eyes magnetic. All eyes were drawn to her.

"Peter, just watch my eyes. Don't turn your head. Watch my eyes and the light. Concentrate on them."

Peter slowly faded into a hypnotic state.

"Peter, you will go on with your story. We know you became addicted to methamphetamine. We know you were arrested. We know you were sentenced to do three years in a correctional facility, until you turned eighteen. You will tell us of your experience in that facility. You will be aware that you are telling us of your experience, and when you wake up, you will remember everything you have told us."

Peter's voice reflected that he was in a trance.

"We got away with what we were doing for a year and a half. One day, a girl named Judy was caught with two hits that I had sold her. She told her parents she bought them from me. They contacted the police. That same week, a kid named Bobby bought some meth that we made. He did the stuff, and then he stole a car. He almost killed two women when the car he stole, smashed head on into theirs. The police busted us, and there were multiple charges. The newspapers played up that we were spoiled Beverly Hills rich kids, and the judge should show us no mercy. We all got the same sentence, but we were sent to different prisons. I was sent to Phillips Correctional. Everyone says that's the worst.

I was bussed to 'Phillips', and put in a large room with seven boys. Two were white, three were black, and two were Mexican. They were all tough looking.

The room was an indoctrination room. We were all wearing blue prison overalls that said, 'Phillips Correctional Institution' on the front.

There were two guards in the room. One was white, and the other black. They were both huge, beefy looking men. I was terrified, and I thought to myself that I better show off how tough I was. It was all an act. The black guard spoke first. 'My name is Officer Clark. At 'Phillips', we keep things on a formal basis. You will speak to the guards with respect at all times. That is Officer Collins. This is your first day at 'Phillips'. Your mug shots have been taken, and you've been issued your uniforms. You will be now be assigned to your rooms. We do not have cells here. We have rooms, with four boys to a room. You will cooperate, and keep your rooms clean. There is no fighting allowed here. If you cause no trouble, you may get out of here unscarred. And when you get out of here, hopefully you will have learned a good lesson. Maybe you can stay out of trouble when you get out'.

I whispered to the boy standing closest to me; 'Yeah if you don't get caught.'

'There is no talking in this room barked Officer Clark'.

I continued my, 'I'm not afraid' routine. 'Come on Officer Clark.'

Officer Clark walked slowly over to where I was seated, and with deliberate calmness, he raised his hand, and backhanded the grin off my face. Then he brutally twisted me around by the shoulders, and read my name.

'Peter Williams. The rich kid, huh? Most of the other boys have been here before. This is your first visit'.

I was crying from the pain and shock as I blurted out, 'My father's going to hear about this. He's got a lot of money! We're not animals.'

Officer Clark then picked me up off the chair by the shirt. His spittle was flying in my face, as his own face showed his fury.

'Fuck you, and fuck your father,' he shouted.

Then Officer Clark punched me viciously in the stomach. I crumbled to the floor.

'You're going to learn some good lessons, you cocksucker. Lick my boot'. Officer Clark held his boot next to my face. I was too scared to move. Then he lifted his other foot to kick me.

I cried, 'No don't.'

He snarled, 'lick my boot faggot'. I licked his boot. I licked and licked, until he just walked away 'Lesson number one. You've got a lot of lessons to learn you punk.'

When indoctrination was over, Officer Clark took me to the room that they assigned me. The room that was going to be my home, for the next three years. The windows all had bars. The door was half solid on the bottom, and the top half had bars for ventilation. At night, the guards let you put a towel over the bars for privacy. There were four cots, four small dressers, and a toilet. Nothing else except my three roommates.

One was a seventeen-year-old, tall skinny white boy with bad acne. The other two were Hispanic. One of them was my age and weight, but he had a lot of muscles and tattoos. The other one was taller."

When Officer Clark shoved me into the room, he told the shorter one, 'I've got a new roommate for you Gonzales. Make sure you show him the ropes.'

'Oh yeah sure Officer Clark,' he answered. 'I'll teach him everything he needs to know'.

Then Officer Clark left, and locked the door.

Gonzales showed me which cot, and which drawers were mine. He told me, 'We keep our crib neat and clean.'

I started to put my few things away, as Gonzales told the white boy to put the towel across the bars.

Gonzales explained to me that the guards can pull it off, but they usually don't.

He asked me what I was in for.

"I said, 'selling meth, how about you?' His one word answer was 'murder.' Then he stood next to me and watched as I put my stuff away. He grabbed a pack of cigarettes out of my hand. When I said, 'those were mine', he punched me in the stomach and I fell to the ground. Then he started to choke me. He had his knee in my back and I couldn't move. I thought I was going to die."

'What you have is mine, white boy, you understand?'

'I understand, I understand.'

'Everything you have is mine.'

"Then the other two joined Gonzales. They tied my hands behind my back with a towel, and threw me facedown on a cot. One boy was stuffing a gag in my mouth, as the other was pulling off my pants. I tried to struggle, but I was helpless. No one heard me crying through the gag, and no one came to help. Gonzales' pants were down, and he started to mount me. I heard him say that, 'Nobody's going to help you, you rich white boy. You're going to be my woman. I'm going to bust you wide open. Then it's Johnny's turn, and then its Boot's turn.'

Gonzales continued to rape me. Oh God it hurt so badly and I felt so ashamed. I felt the cot moving as Gonzales whispered in my ear; 'We going to take you every night. Anyway we want to woman. You're going to keep the crib clean, woman. You going to do anything we want, woman.' As he climaxed in me he kept chanting woman. Then he turned me over to Johnny, and then to Boot.

16

They keep raping me all night. They told me if I complain, Clark wouldn't do anything any way, but they would kill me. They kept raping me. It hurts so badly."

Peter is crying now while still under hypnosis.

"I couldn't do anything, but what they wanted me to do."

Everyone was staring at Peter, mesmerized by his story.

Dr. Crawford pushed on, "How long did this go on?"

"For a few hours the first night. Then every night for the next nine months. Everybody knew! Even the guards, but nobody cared. They all fucked me!

They made me blow them. I cleaned the crib. I was their woman. They didn't have to force me, it was useless to resist. They even made me tell them that I love them, and I wanted more. It continued on, and then I got sick. I almost died from an infection. I really wanted to die. I was too ashamed to tell my father. I felt so dirty.

He found out from the doctor, and the prison Chaplin. He got his lawyers to get me an early release. Now I'm here."

Suddenly, a light started to flash on the arm of Dr. Crawford's desk, signaling her to pick up her phone. She asked if it was an emergency.

"I understand. I'll be there shortly."

The lights came up in the room.

"You will wake up Peter, when I count to three. You will remember all that you've told us. You will remember that you've told it all to us. We, as a group will help you deal with your wounds, and help you to heal. One, two, three. I have to go now. There's a young girl in crisis at Westwood General Hospital. The poor child attempted suicide. Only something this urgent would pull me away right now."

CHAPTER FIVE

D r. Crawford walked into a private hospital room, and saw a very frail looking, but lovely, blond-haired girl in the hospital bed. She was shackled to the bed with arm and leg restraints. There was a pretty young nurse in attendance. Dr. Crawford ordered the nurse to show her the girl's charts. Then she snapped at the subdued nurse, "Why is this child in restraints? Remove them at once."

The nurse moved to comply, but explained, "Dr. Crawford, it was standard procedure. She tried to slash her wrists."

"This is Dr. Vargas's daughter. There is nothing standard about this. Do you know who Dr. Vargas is?"

"I know he's a surgeon at California General."

"He's not just a surgeon. He's a noted brain surgeon and Chief of Surgery at California General. Please leave us alone."

The nurse left and Doctor Crawford sat down on the bed next to Susie. She took her pencil flashlight and clipped it to her belt. It was a familiar ritual.

There was something that about this patient that touched Dr. Crawford's heart. She looked pretty and vulnerable. She could have been the daughter that she never had.

Then, she took Susie's hand with care and tenderness.

"Suzanne Vargas or do you prefer Susie, Sue, or something else?"

When she got no response she continued.

"My name is Dr. Crawford, Suzanne. Since I don't know if you have any other preference, I will call you Suzanne. My name is Mary. Mary Crawford. But I will always insist on being called Dr. Crawford."

When Susie still didn't respond, Dr. Crawford continued "Very well, Suzanne. Do you know why I'm here?"

"You're here because I tried to kill myself. You're here because you want to change my mind. Well, you won't!"

"Suzanne, according to your records you were raped. You feel dirty and degraded, and that you've let your father down. You feel unworthy. You just want to end it all."

"That's right, and you can't stop me."

"Well, I'm not going to let you kill yourself. You told me why you're here, but do you know why it's me that's been called?"

"No"

"Your father is a very important man in the medical profession. They called me because I'm the best. The very best in suicide prevention. You will not commit suicide. I'm going to help you deal with the feelings you have. Suzanne, I'm going to be your friend, you'll see. I'm going to go now. You'll be here for about two weeks. If you try to kill yourself while you're here, that's unwise. They have the equipment to bring you back. They will save your life, and then restrain you again. So you might as well give me my two weeks, Suzanne. You may decide that living is a better solution to your problem than dying is."

That evening, Dr. Crawford was in Dr. Vargas's office. He was a fifty-year-old, six-feet tall man and in good physical shape. He was not an attractive man, and he was very abrupt.

"I do appreciate your paying attention to my daughter. So often our patients look to us as though we are God. I sometimes feel like I'm God. But when it's my own daughter, I'm just a terrified father."

Dr. Crawford asked Dr. Vargas for whatever details he could provide.

"Susie's mother died soon after giving birth to her. She was suffering from postpartum depression, and committed suicide. I never remarried my work you know. I raised Susie myself.

"Susie was raped four weeks ago. It was a violent rape. Her attacker tied her up,"

Dr. Crawford gave him a glass of water, as Dr. Vargas started to choke with emotion. He continued. "Her attacker lured her somehow into his car. Then he blindfolded her, and drove her to a cabin in the woods. He raped, beat, and sodomized her for hours. The medical report tells us all that. Then he just let her go, after he called her a filthy whore. He has not been caught, and Susie blames herself."

"Dr. Vargas, I may use hypnosis on her. It often is a valuable tool."

"She may not be a good subject for hypnosis, my dear. In my work I take infinite interest in the workings of the brain. I do a lot of biochemical research in my own private laboratory, in the basement of my home. I'll tell you about it at a later time, if you're interested."

"I'm very interested, Doctor."

"Yes well Susie has injected a substance that may block or inhibit hypnosis. It also may contribute to her feelings of guilt. Please, Doctor, do your best for my Susie. I have to leave for my laboratory now. I am at a crucial point in an experiment.

Doctor, the usual protocol is to keep Suzanne under observation here at Westwood General for two weeks. I'm going to order her released with instructions that she must receive treatment at my office on a prescribed schedule.

I know I leave my daughter in your very capable and lovely hands."

Dr. Vargas kissed Dr. Crawford's hand in courtly European fashion, and then turned and reached for the door.

CHAPTER SIX

It was late afternoon of the next day, as Dr. Crawford addressed the group.

"Yesterday, we explored Peter's situation. Today we will delve into Andrew's situation."

Andrew was sixteen years old, acted very self-assured, and came from a very affluent home.

"I don't mind talking about my problem. My older brother, Mike, has done acid for the last ten years. He let me try it when I was twelve, and I've been doing it ever since.

The big problem happened when I left a paper with a hundred hits on it. My little sister Laurie is only three. She got a hold of it, and ate some. She flipped out, and they don't know if she'll ever be the same."

The lights on Dr, Crawford's chair started to flicker.

"Hold that thought, Andrew," Dr. Crawford said as she answered her phone.

"Hey I'm through anyway"

She smiled at Andrew. Her smile conveyed compassion, and understanding.

"No Andrew, you're far from being through."

Now Dr. Crawford spoke into the phone "Are you sure? Will he live? Is there brain damage? No it won't take me long to get there.'

She disconnected, and explained to the group.

"This is very unusual. First yesterday's emergency, and now to-night. But I must rush off to Westwood General again. A young man overdosed on cocaine tonight. He's out of danger now, but I must see him right away. He'll be joining our group. He'll be a little older member for the group."

"How do you know he'll join us?"

"Because I'm good at what I do, David. In fact, I'm the best. I might just hypnotize him, and make him join."

Their eyes met, and held each other for several seconds.

CHAPTER SEVEN

The hospital room was much like the room that Susie had at Westwood General. Karl was a thirty-five-year old man. He had long black hair, and was very thin and wiry. He was lying in his bed with no restraints. Dr. Crawford was dressed in a business suit. She sat in a chair beside Karl as she asked him, "Mr. Berber? Do you know who I am?"

"You're probably a shrink or a nark." Karl's answer conveyed antagonism, and distrust.

Dr. Crawford smiled slightly, as she took out her small pencil flashlight and clipped it to her breast pocket.

"What's that a microphone?"

"No, Karl, I'm not a narc, and that's not a microphone. Would you care to see it up close?"

She handed the flashlight to Karl. He turned it on and off and examined it, as if it might be dangerous. Satisfied he handed it back.

"I am a shrink. Do you know why I'm here?"

Karl answered, "I don't like shrinks, and I don't need one".

"Some people might think different. You overdosed on crack tonight. You do need help."

"I don't remember. I don't remember any of that crap. Besides, I don't do crack. I probably had amnesia, and just because I ride a Harley, you think I do drugs."

Dr. Crawford waited a moment, and then answered.

"Karl, I'll tell you what I do know. Some of it you'll probably tell me yourself, but this much I already know. Two days ago your fiancée, Terri Lane, broke up with you. You, and she had argued over your addiction, and she left you. She figures you spent the last two days doing heavy crack smoking."

Karl snapped at her, "Terri had nothing to do with it."

"Be quiet! Terri came back to your apartment a few hours ago. You were lying on the floor stiff. You weren't breathing. There was a hot crack pipe on the floor next to you. The rug had just started to smolder. Terri guessed you'd had a seizure, so she called nine-one-one... She threw away all the drugs and paraphernalia, so you wouldn't get arrested. Then she came to the hospital, and waited outside. The hospital called me.

Terri told me all this. She still loves you, Karl, although I don't know why."

"Terri's here? She still loves me? I don't want to lose her Miss."

"It's Doctor Crawford."

"I don't want to lose her. Where is she?"

"She doesn't want to see you. Not right now. If you put the pipe down, then you may have a chance with her."

"It's not easy. I'm hooked Dr. Crawford. God, it's got me by the balls."

"That's what I meant when I said, part of this you will tell me. One, are you ready to stop? And two, do you have health insurance to cover the cost of treatment?"

"I have insurance from my job. I do work you know."

"And Karl, do you want to stop smoking crack?"

"I love Terri. I'd stop breathing for her. Yes, I want to stop."

Later that evening Dr. Crawford met with Terri Lane. She was a lovely, red haired woman of thirty two.

"I can help him," Dr. Crawford explained, "but it won't be easy. Give him encouragement, but don't give in. Let him know that if he stays clean, and in treatment, that you might marry him. His emotions are going to pay havoc with him. Crack does that. You have to stay strong for him. I've hypnotized him, and left him with a strong hypnotic suggestion. He can go home tonight. There is nothing more to be done here. He must then join my therapy session tomorrow. I've given him the address, and time. I have to go, and see another patient now. Take care of yourself, dear. This will not be easy for you."

Dr. Crawford rushed back to Westwood General to see Susie. Her immediate strategy was to get Susie to trust, and even to love her. She brought her flowers, and adjusted her bed. She gave her water, smoothed her hair, and whispered something funny in her ear. Susie giggled, as she decompressed a little.

"Suzanne, I've arranged for your release from the hospital for tomorrow. You won't have to spend the two weeks here, so long as you're under my care. Here is my card. It's very important that you come by my office tomorrow afternoon at four o'clock."

Then Dr. Crawford dimmed the lights, tucked her in, and gently told her to try to sleep now. Dr Crawford gave Susie a motherly kiss on the forehead, and walked out the door.

CHAPTER EIGHT

The following afternoon, Dr. Crawford walked into her office. After greeting her secretary, she sorted through her mail. It was a daily routine.

"Doctor, your group is all here. Mr. Berber has joined the group, and they're waiting in their respective chairs. Also, Suzanne called. She will be here at four o'clock."

"Have you heard from the telephone company yet? I still see the same shady looking character hanging around. I really have to report this to the police."

Dr. Crawford didn't wait for an answer. She just turned and entered the therapy room.

"Good afternoon. We have a new member joining our group today. Please introduce yourself."

"I feel kind of awkward. These kids are kind of young."

"They've all had problems as adult as yours. This is a group challenge. When we face our addictions as a group, we gain strength. You will benefit from the others, since they have been in therapy longer. And they can benefit from you, since you are older. Welcome, Karl."

The therapy session lasted two hours without interruption. During it, Dr Crawford placed Andrew in a hypnotic state. It became evident that Andrew didn't understand the gravity, or didn't care that his sister might be damaged for life. Notes were made that Andrew was showing psychopathic tendencies, and might need intense private treatment.   Next Dr. Crawford hypnotized fifteen-year-old Peggy. Under hypnosis, it was learned that Peggy was trying to escape from her belief that she was worthless, ugly, and totally unloved. She had always been very overweight, and was teased by her schoolmates since the first grade. Even her parents, who paid much more attention to her older brother and younger sister, would call her, "Humpty Dumpty." She had become withdrawn. She did poorly at school. And she had given up. She just didn't want to feel the pain anymore. Money was always left lying around her house. Her father made so much money, that he didn't treat it with respect. She could easily take a ten, or twenty dollar bill, with no one noticing. The internet was a wonderful tool. You could learn almost everything on it, including how to use heroin. There was a man who hung out at her school. Everyone knew he sold the stuff, and the needle that went with it.

The first time she used it, it was fantastic. She was finally able to not care what the rest of the world thought of her. She could just relax, and float on air. For the first time that she could remember, she felt no pain. By the second time she used it, she was hooked. She shot up daily, for the next three months. Nobody noticed, and nobody cared. Until one day when she overdosed. If a maid hadn't gone into her room, she would have died. If the maid hadn't noticed that she had drool coming from her mouth, she would have died. And if the maid hadn't realized that she could not wake Peggy up, she would have died. The world finally noticed Peggy. Enrolling Peggy in the group therapy sessions was an excellent way for her parents to shift the responsibility away from themselves.

Dr. Crawford had weeks before determined that Jeffery was no longer at risk. And without his influence, Valarie did not need much work. Just hearing the consequences of the other group member's addictions, is getting her ready for her hypnosis sessions.

The other business of the session was, with the help of hypnosis, to make Karl feel more comfortable with the other members of the group.

The group session ended promptly at three, and Susie arrived promptly at four. The therapy room was now arranged for Susie. The lights were lowered, and there was soothing music playing softly in the background. Dr. Crawford and Susie were seated in two identical cushioned chairs facing each other.

Susie was a very special client. She has somehow touched Dr. Crawford's heart in a way that none of her other clients had.

An additional motivation was that her father was a famous and highly respected brain surgeon. Saving his daughter's life would be an important chapter in her next book.

The plan of treatment would be gentle, and could take as long as two years. This first session lasted an hour.

"This was a very good beginning, Suzanne. Do you feel better at all?"

"I feel a little better, but that's not unusual. Some days I feel better, and then some days the depression lays over me like a blanket. I feel like it's smothering me. I feel like the only peace I can get is with death."

"Suzanne, depression is caused by chemical impulses that control certain secretions in the base of your pituitary gland. Because there has been no research done on interactions that might occur with some of the medications that your father gave you, you're not a good subject for hypnosis.

When your depression starts to overwhelm you, call me. I'm going to give you four telephone numbers to call me on. One is the office, one is the hospital, one is my answering service, and one is my home. If you feel bad you can always reach me. Your treatment will not be quick, but little by little it will get better. I'm not going to let this tragedy ruin your life. When ever you feel the need to call me, call. And always remember that I love you, and I will always be there for you"

"Dr Crawford, everybody calls me Susie."

"Very well, from now on, Susie it shall be."

CHAPTER NINE

It had sort of become a tradition. After each group session, all members of the group went to "Duke's."

Duke's, was an upscale coffee shop, about three blocks from Dr. Crawford's office. There were a few tables up front, which looked out on the street. There was a dance floor behind the front tables with an old fashioned juke box. Then there were small booths behind the juke box. The front tables were moveable, and could be combined to accommodate up to twelve people. The group went there for light refreshments, and to further their camaraderie.

The group took their usual table with a view of the street, and said their hello's to Duke.

Duke was a bear of a man. He was forty years of age, and had a very affable temperament. He always had a smile and an enthusiastic greeting for all his regulars.

"Hello, kids. I see you've brought a new recruit today."

Karl was surprised... "He knows?"

David answered, "We come here all the time. Duke is super cool. He's heard us talk, and fool around, but he really doesn't know details."

"I think Duke is cute," Valarie joined in, "in a fatherly type of way."

Peter added, "Well he's old enough to be your father."

"So what?" she answered.

Karl entered the banter, "Dr. Crawford seems to like young men."

Andrew asked, "What do you mean Karl?"

"She's got the hots for David here."

David was surprised, "No way, man. She's our doctor."

"In case you haven't noticed, she's a woman, too."

The chatter died away, as the group finished coffee and ice cream. They parted and went their separate ways.

It had been three months since Karl's first session. The therapy was progressing well with everyone.

Susie's fits of suicidal depression were still intense, but less frequent. The rest of the group was starting to mend, to individual degrees. Andrew got no better, but no worse. Valarie and Jeffrey were easy. Through hypnosis their addictive need for cocaine was diminishing. Karl was the most difficult, but there had been break-throughs.

This evening, Karl rode his Harley Davidson Roadster to meet with Terri. He parked at the curb, and started to tell Terri about his day. Two young men were sitting on their bikes next to Karl. They were both grungy, and were wearing the colors of the same motorcycle gang that Karl was wearing. Three biker girls pulled up next to the men. The girls were wearing very tight shorts. They were wearing low buttoned shirts, with lots of breast in view.

They were pretty, and very sexy looking. The men revved up their engines.

"Come on, Karl! We ain't going to wait forever!"

The second biker added, "Man, if your bitch don't like to party, I'll give you mine."

The girl sitting next to him on her bike was laughing and shaking her breasts to show more of what she had.

"Just wait a fucking minute, man." Karl swung off his bike. His jeans were skin tight as he walked over to Terri. He looked lean and mean. His hair was unruly, and he had a gold earring in one ear.

Terri was dressed conservatively. Even though she was not trying to look sexy, she was still very sexy, and very beautiful. Karl took her hand in a way that was kind of rough, and led her down the block, away from the others.

"Terri, don't you see what you're doing to me?"

"Karl, you're hurting me."

"It's been three months now. Three months, that I've been seeing that bitch. Three months that I've been clean."

"She's not a bitch. Dr. Crawford is an expert, and she's helping you Karl."

"Terri, I'm not talking about me. I'm talking about us."

One of the two bikers called to Karl; "Hey, Karl, we're going to the house. Bring your old lady, or come alone. It's your trip."

The bikes peeled off. They did wheelies, and just missed an elderly couple crossing the street.

"Those crazy bastards are beautiful. Terri, are you my old lady or not?"

"No, Karl. I'm not your old lady, and I never was. I'm your girlfriend, and I still don't know if that's going to work out. I will not go along with your biker gang, old lady mentality. Ever since you started riding with them, our problems started. You never used to get high before. You always made me feel like your woman, and that made me feel good. When you're with them you make me feel like I'm your bitch. It's degrading."

"Come on Terri, they're my friends. I can still keep my friends, and not get high. You'll see."

"I don't like your friends, and when you're around them, I don't even like you. And don't give up crack for me. Give it up for yourself."

"Terri, I can't have you. You won't move back in with me. I can't have any friends. What do you want me to have?"

"Love for yourself" Terri snapped. "That's first. Then love and respect for me. As long as you still want to get high, you don't love yourself. And as long as you keep the company that you keep, you show me that you don't respect me either. I'm not sure that you know what love is."

Terri walked away in anger.

CHAPTER TEN

It had been two nights since Terri and Karl's confrontation. That night's therapy session was dedicated to exploring the fight. The lights had been lowered. Every so often, David glanced at Dr. Crawford, and Dr. Crawford caught his eye. There was a subtle undercurrent of attraction.

Karl was up to the point in the story where Terri was leaving. "Then she just walked away."

"Karl when did this happen?"

"The other night, after the session, after we all left Duke's. I called Terri, and asked her to meet me."

"And then what happened?"

Karl was so intent in telling the story, that he was not aware of Dr. Crawford turning on her pencil flashlight. The action caused Karl to drift into a state of hypnosis. Dr. Crawford had programmed that reaction into Karl at an earlier session. He was in a trance, when he responded to her next question.

"And then what happened?"

"I watched her walk away, and turn the corner. I couldn't move for a minute. She was gone, and I started to scream to the wind. All right then, I don't care. I don't care. I felt so defeated, that I kept screaming to no one, until my throat was raw. Then I just got on my bike, and turned around to follow my brothers."

Dr. Crawford instructed Karl to describe the club house.

"The house is a loft, in a deserted home, overlooking the street. It has one window that is covered with a blanket. The street used to be a mixture of nice small houses, and cool shops. It got run down and rough. Nobody wanted to come into the neighborhood to shop, so the shops just closed up. The houses on the street, started to go downhill. People stopped wanting to walk past the drunks sleeping on the street. It is a perfect place for us. Nobody cares what we do. And if they care, they are too scared of us to complain. There is a small stove, a small refrigerator, and a sink in one corner of the nine hundred square foot room. There are a couple of old stuffed chairs. There are two mattresses on the floor. There is a swing chair hanging from the ceiling. There is a sound system, to play tapes on. There is one shaded light that hangs from the ceiling. And one shaded lamp on the floor.

The door to enter and leave is double bolted, and there is also a police security lock. The paint on the walls, which was once white, has a film of residue from all of the crack smoke. There is dirt, and mess everywhere. There are four posters on the wall. One is of a Harley Davidson motorcycle. Two are soft porn, and one depicts a naked girl straddling the extended tailpipe of a motorcycle, as if it was a man's penis.

When I got there the other night, there were crack pipes all over the room. The garbage was overflowing, with empty beer cans. There were nine people, besides me.

No one had paired up yet. Two brothers were on a mattress, with one sister. On another mattress, there was one brother with two females. One sister was sitting naked in the swing chair. One brother was cooking up a fresh batch of crack. The other was just standing, and staring at the blanket on the window.

I sat on a couch, and watched all this. Everyone else was stoned. I was the only one not smoking crack.

The two men, with the one sister, passed their crack pipe and torch back and forth between them. The two sisters with the one brother, also shared one pipe, but they were shot gunning the smoke. One bitch did a hit, and then put her mouth on the other bitches open mouth, and exhaled the smoke into it. When the girls shot gunned each other, it turned me on. I watched as their lips stayed together, while their tongues touched.

Then the sister on the swing chair took a big hit of crack. She leaned her head back, and spread her legs over the front of the chair.

She then let the swinging chair take her to some place called ecstasy.

"All of a sudden the blanket dude hit his pipe, and then he turned to me, and offered me the pipe. I looked around the room. My jacket was on the floor.

He was shirtless. The swing girl is nude. All the other sisters are topless, and were down to their panties. The other brothers were wearing shorts.

"God, I wanted to take the pipe he offered me. He kept on insisting that I take the pipe. Finally I turned away from him. I was war with myself. I wanted it, but I didn't want it.

Then one of my brothers walked up to me. He did a big hit, and blew the smoke in my face." 'Come on Karl. It's been weeks already, since the last time you got high.'

'No, man, I'm still not ready. I don't want to do any.'

'Man you are a real buzz killer.'

Then the other brother called out, so everybody heard him, 'Fuck him. There's more for us.'

I got up, and just got ready to split. Just then the other brother loaded up his pipe, and put it down in front of me with a torch and a lighter. As he walked away he said, 'maybe you ought to just do a hit.'

I just stood there. I felt like my legs were frozen in place. I was about to give in when one of the sisters, who was giving shot guns got up. Her legs were long. Her stomach was flat and her breasts were high and firm. She lit the torch, and did the hit. Then while she was holding the smoke in, she pushed me into the chair, and she straddled me. She kissed my neck, and rubbed my chest with her hands. Then she put her mouth by mine.

'Take the smoke baby.'

I pushed her away and said, 'no! I've got to get the hell out of here.' I grabbed my jacket, and rushed for the door. A brother tried to stop me, but I shoved him out of my way."

As Karl was brought out of the trance he asked to no one, "How much more can I do for her?"

Dr. Crawford brought the light up in the room.

"It's not what you do for her, Karl. It's what you do for yourself."

"No, it's for her. Why can't she see that?"

"She does see that, Karl. That's the problem. Some days you'll fight. Everyone does, or you'll take her for granted. Or she'll take you for granted. Someday, even for just a little while, you may not want to do this for Terri. What will happen then?"

"I don't know. I'll stay clean, anyway."

"Will you Karl? Terri is not so sure, and it scares the hell out of her. She loves you, and if she commits to you, she couldn't cope with it if you picked up the pipe again. She would blame you, and hate herself. She knows there are no guarantees, but she also knows that you have to want to stay clean. Only then can you claim yourself, and there's a chance, that you will stay clean."

CHAPTER 11

D r Crawford announced that the group would meet again on
Friday, and asked David to stay behind.

Peter walked over to David.

"What does Dr. Crawford want you to stay for?"

"I don't know. I'll see you guys at Duke's in a few minutes."

David called to Karl, as he was walking out the door.

"Hey Karl, are you going to Duke's?"

"Yeah buddy. I'll see you there."

The rest of the group left. Dr. Crawford walked into the outer
office, and locked the door. She then returned to the therapy room.
David was standing there, watching as she straightened the chairs.
They both seemed a little uncomfortable, as she turned to face him.

She used a commanding tone, as she told David to sit in his
chair. David obeyed.

"Do you remember when I first found you, David?"

"Yes, Dr. Crawford. I was strung out on crack. I was homeless.
I guess I was headed for jail. Or maybe I guess I was pretty close
to killing myself, or someone else. I was so scared all the time. It

had all gotten out of control. I hated myself, but I couldn't stop. I couldn't change."

"And now David?"

"I've been clean for nine months. I got a job driving a forklift. I have my own small pad. And I have my own car. It's pretty good now."

"And I did it for you! I got you to stay clean. I used my influence so you could get the job. You pay your own rent, but I paid for your apartment until you could. Do you know why, David?"

"No, Dr. Crawford, I guess I don't."

"Peter's father is a wealthy accountant. Andrew's father owns three McDonald's restaurants, and he's quite well off. Jeffrey and Valarie's mother is an actress. She is the star of a soap opera, and has made a fortune doing commercials. And Peggy's parents just want to not have any responsibility in her life. They're willing to pay any amount of money to get Peggy out of their hair. Do you get the picture David? Everyone in the group pays me a lot of money. Even your friend Karl. His insurance pays me well. You have no parents. You can't pay me."

David was panicked at the thought of leaving the group.

"What do you want, Dr. Crawford? I could try to pay you something. I would do anything."

"I want you to treat me with respect."

"I do respect you, Dr. Crawford. I never talk back or anything."

"You look at me, like I'm someone you hope to score. I'm your doctor David!"

David looked uncomfortable and even embarrassed. He looked vulnerable, and Dr. Crawford started to feel sorry for him.

"I really thought that you liked me."

She reached over and gently touched David's cheek.

"I do like you, David. I like you, as though you were my son. David, it's important that we get this out, and deal with it. I can't allow you to think of me as some kind of potential conquest."

"I don't think of you that way."

"Then just how do you think of me?"

"Dr. Crawford, I think I love you."

Suddenly the door from the office opened. Dr. Crawford was startled, and so was the sixty-year-old cleaning woman.

"I'm from the Ready Maid cleaning service. I'm sorry if I interrupted you ma'am. I thought I would get an early start. They said no one would be here tonight."

"My schedule can always change! Just start on the front office."

"Yes, ma'am."

CHAPTER TWELVE

It was an hour and twenty minutes later, when David walked into Duke's. Duke was behind the counter. Of the group, only Karl and Terri were still there as David joined them.

"Hey, Karl, where did everyone go?"

"Peter's father and Valarie's mother came tonight, and they had to leave early. Then every one else left"

David greeted Terri, as she smiled back at David.

Karl asked David, "What took so long?"

"Dr. Crawford wanted to talk to me about a bunch of things. How long have you and Terri known each other?"

Terri answered that they met at a dance contest.

"A dance contest? You, Karl?"

"Yeah, we used to be good too. I mean really good."

"What kind of dancing did you guys do?"

Terri answered, "Exhibition ballroom. We both used to dance at the School of Performing Arts."

"Wow, that's incredible."

Karl proudly added, "We won a 1986 Future Star Quest contest."

"Let's show David some steps, Karl."

Karl was very reluctant, as he tried to get out of it gracefully. "Naw Duke wouldn't have that kind of music on his juke box."

"I bet he does," added David. "He has some songs that say standard oldies."

Terri went to check out the selections and called out, "Honey, they have Dancing in the Dark." She put a quarter in the slot for it to start. While the jukebox moved to the selection, she rushed over and took Karl's hand. Not too reluctantly Karl followed her, and then held her in a dance position. The music started, and Terri closed her eyes, as she pictured what used to be. She swayed in Karl's arms as she remembered the announcer proclaim, "Our Future Star Quest winners will now dance for our TV audience."

In her reverie she saw a clean cut Karl, with the two of them wearing beautiful clothes, as they danced a wonderful routine. The looks that went back and forth between them could not be confused with anything else except love. The dance ended with Karl dipping Terri. Terri's face had a momentary look of rapture and tears of joy that turned to tears of sadness, at the reality of what they had lost.

As they headed back to join David, Karl asked Terri why she was crying.

"We had it all, Karl. We really had it all until you started to get high."

As they sat down David was bubbling over with praise.

"That was great you two. I mean really great."

Karl didn't try to hide the disappointment in himself, "We used to have it going for us."

"Dr. Crawford's going to help you to get it all back," David promised.

"David, I wonder about her. Sometimes I don't trust her."

"Karl, that's not fair," Terri reminded him. "Look at how much good she has done for you so far."

"She's done well for everyone," David added. "I especially owe her."

Terri asked, "How do you figure that, David?"

"She gets money from everyone else. She helps me just because she wants to. I owe it to her to stay straight, even when I don't want to."

"Let me tell you how it is, my young buddy. You don't owe her anything. In fact, you don't owe anybody anything. You're right; she makes money off every one of us. Especially on the private sessions. So forget her shit. You've got to stay straight for you. You, yourself.

She's got her reasons for taking you on as a freebie. Maybe to ease her conscience for making money off people like us. Or maybe she just likes you."

"What do you mean, she just likes me?"

"I mean, maybe she's got the hots for you."

Terri chimed in, "I don't think you're being fair, Karl! But it does sound like some of Dr. Crawford's ideas are getting through to you."

"What do you mean?"

"Well sweetheart, what you just told David, about doing his sobriety for himself. That's what Dr. Crawford first told you."

Karl's mood had turned combative. "A lot of good it does me! Move back in with me, Terri."

"No, not yet."

"That's what I mean. I want to marry you Terri. I want for us to sleep together again. But it's no good with you. What good does all this do me?"

"I'm still here, Karl. I wouldn't be if you were still getting high. I want the same things that you want. I want to marry you, and to sleep with you, and to hold you in my arms all night. But you're not ready yet. Or maybe I'm not ready yet. No really, you're not ready yet."

Terri was now visibly upset She was about to cry, as she got up.

"I have to go now. I love you, Karl. I'll see you tomorrow night. Maybe we can go to a movie."

Terri kissed Karl and rushed out the door. Both men watched her until she was out of sight.

"Damn, David! There's no winning with her. She's got to give me more. Can't she see that?"

David did not know what to say. He wished he could help his friend.

"Listen David, I've got to go and get a little cash from one of the guys at my club. He owes it to me. Do you want to come along?"

"Yeah great, I've never seen your clubhouse."

"It's not so great."

It only took about thirty minutes for the two young men get to the front of the club. Karl parked his Harley next to five other bikes by the curb. David was sitting behind Karl, and as they dismounted Karl pointed out the blanket covered window. They walked in the bottom door, and up the dimly lit staircase. When they got to the wooden door of the loft, Karl knocked three times, and then twice.

"They don't open the door unless you knock three, and then two times. Then you have to give the right answer to the question."

"Who are you here to see?" a voice asked.

"Karl answered, "B-four." Locks opened, and the door opened. Inside there was one biker from before, sitting by himself on a chair, smoking crack. On the other side of the room, two mattresses had been pulled together. Four men and two women were sitting on them in a circle, passing a pipe. There was a pile of beer cans on the floor. The one biker, who was smoking alone, called to get Karl's attention. As Karl, with David in tow, approached Snap they noticed a German shepherd puppy tied to the chair. David's eyes were everywhere.

"Wow Karl, this place is cool."

Karl didn't answer David. Snap was just starting a hit on the pipe as they reached him. David's eyes were fixed on the pipe. He was mesmerized by it. Karl also watched Snap. He had a hard time looking away, but he did, and he turned his attention to the puppy.

"Where did you get the dog, and why do you have him up here?"

Snap took another hit, and he blew the smoke at the puppy.

"The dogs a head man she loves the stuff. She's my new smoking partner. That is, since you don't smoke. She's a better partner than you. She smokes's less, bitches less, and she smells a hell of a lot better then you." Snap laughed at his own joke.

Karl petted the puppy, and tells Snap, "That's fucked, man. Leave the dog alone."

Snap offered the pipe to Karl. "Karl, do you want a hit?"

Karl hesitated, because right then there was nothing he wanted more.

"No man no, I'm off the stuff. I came to pick up the ten bucks you owe me."

Snap leaned over to David, and loaded the pipe with a big hit.

"I can't offer you any. Karl is a homeboy, and this is my own private stash. This isn't a party night."

"Snap, do you have my money?"

"Yeah man, just give me a minute." He leaned over to David, "I'll sell you a hit for five dollars."

"No thanks. I'd better not."

"Come on Snap. If you've got the money give it to me."

Snap looked in his pockets, but came up empty.

"Give me a minute brother. It's got to be in my other jacket." Snap loaded two pipes. He put one down, and lit the other. "Five bucks and you can do that one."

David couldn't resist. "I'm going to do it," as he pulled out a five dollar bill.

"No David, don't."

David handed Snap the five dollars. "Karl just one okay. I can do just one hit, and then we'll go."

David reached for the pipe, but Karl grabbed him viciously by the arm, and pulled him away. "No, Goddamn it! I'm not going to let you."

"He paid for it. No refunds."

"Keep the fucking five, Snap, and forget the ten you owe me too!"

Karl forced David out the door, and down onto the street.

"I can't believe it. I would have done it. I couldn't stop myself."

"Are you all right, man? I hope I didn't hurt your arm."

"You're strong Karl, but you didn't hurt me. And thanks, I wouldn't just stop at one hit. I knew it even as I said it."

"I shouldn't have brought you with me. I was stupid. I'm sorry, David."

CHAPTER THIRTEEN

I t was morning, a week after David's near slip. Sharon was seated at her desk. Dr. Crawford was sitting on the edge of her own desk.

She was wearing a tight fitting suit, with a row of buttons up the side of the skirt. Dr. Crawford had a lot of buttons open, showing a lot of leg. It was a very sexy outfit.

"Your schedule is fairly light today. At one o'clock your appointment is set with Mr. Brown. Suzanne will be here at three o'clock. At five you have a new patient. Her name is Betty Walters. She's been suffering from depression, and she's afraid she's going to hurt her baby."

"What are the financial arrangements?"

"It's a compensation case, Doctor. It's alleged that the depression stems from work induced pressure."

"Good."

"At eight o'clock tonight David comes in. Will you want me to stay while David is here?"

Dr. Crawford was very preoccupied with thoughts of the coming night. She didn't remember Betty's last name.

"No, Sharon. When Betty what's her last name leaves, you can go also."

Sharon thought that something must be bothering her boss. It was unusual for her to forget a patient's last name. "And Sharon, cancel that Ready Maid cleaning service. Start someone new next week."

Dr. Crawford got up, pulled up a chair by her desk, and started doing her paper work.

At that moment, Susie was also sitting by her desk in her own room. The sun was coming through her blinds. Her room was small and neat. Dr. Vargas was out of town at a convention in Las Vegas, and she was writing a letter to him.

"Dear Daddy,

I'm having a really bad day. Some days are better. This day is really, really, bad.

I keep thinking back to the day I was raped. What did I do to cause it? What could I have done to stop it? How could I have avoided it?

Susie started reliving that day in her memory. She envisions herself on that pleasant spring day, when she was walking down the street in Westwood Village, as if it's happening now.

She is dressed in shorts and a peasant blouse. She is walking alone, window shopping in the trendy stores on the street. She doesn't notice the forty-five-year old man watching her. The man's hair is dark, and he is about five feet, ten inches tall. He weighs around one hundred and eighty pounds. His hair is slightly long, and he is dressed in casual clothes. He's doing nothing that makes him seem potentially dangerous. As Susie turns away from a window, the man walks up to her. He has one hand in a pocket.

"Excuse me, miss do you know where Gaily Avenue is?" His question and manor are not threatening.

"Gaily is just four blocks from here. If you just walk"

Suddenly, the man grabs her arm, and steps close to her, as he pulls a knife out of his pocket. "Make a sound, and I'll cut you! Listen carefully. First, I'll slash your face, and then I'll cut your throat."

Susie is terrified and afraid to scream. She looks left and right, but no one is coming towards them.

The man tightens his hold on Susie's arm. "Even if you don't die, you'll be scarred for life. Listen to me. I won't hurt you. Come with me to my car."

He pulls her over to his car. Susie is too afraid to try to fight back. He opens the car door, and pushes her inside. Then he slides in next to her. The cars windows are tinted, so no one can see the inside, from the outside. He puts the knife against her throat. "Put your hands behind your back."

"Please don't hurt me," Susie cries.

He twists her arm as he says, "If you obey me, I won't hurt you. Now do it. Put your hands behind your back."

Crying from fear and pain, Susie obeys. The man twists a rope around her wrists, and ties her hands. Then he reaches past her, and takes out a roll of adhesive tape from the glove compartment. He tears off a piece, and puts it over her mouth. Then he tears off another piece, and covers her eyes.

Then he drives her to a little cabin in Palmdale. It has one room, and the window is boarded over. The walls and doors are insulated for soundproofing. He takes off his own clothing and rips off Susie's clothing. She only has on her bikini panties. Her hands are still tied, but the tape is off her mouth and eyes. The man is holding a riding crop in his hand. He starts to hit her all over her body with the crop, raising red welts, on her legs and back.

Susie screams as he hits her again on the legs.

He enjoys hearing her scream, as with each blow he repeats, "Scream some more bitch. Nobody can hear a sound outside. You're a filthy bitch."

Susie is terrified and whimpering.

"Tell me you like me to whip you," As he raises the crop, "Tell me tell me."

Susie cringes and quietly says, "I like you to whip me."

"You're like a bitch dog! A filthy bitch dog."

He then grabs Susie by the hair and rips off her panties.

"You love me." he is ranting. "You love me. Tell me that you love me, and then tell me again."

Now, the fiend holds up a dog's leash and chocker chain.

"You walk over here my bitch dog. You're going to put on your leash and collar."

Susie is frozen in fear. She can't move forward, or back away.

He steps up to her, and puts his face so close that it touches her face. "You're going to put this collar on. You're going to walk on your knees. You're going to crawl. I'm going to beat you, and choke you."

"No. Please God, no. I'm a good girl. No I beg of you."

The man raises the crop again, and Susie puts the chocker on over her head.

"You're going to beg me to take you like a bitch dog."

Meanwhile, back in Dr. Crawford's office it was fifteen minutes past three.

"Dr. Crawford, Susie called while you were with Mr. Brown."

"Sharon, did she say what she wanted?"

"She asked to speak to you, and she sounded a little upset. I told her you were with a client. She said not to disturb you, and that she wouldn't be in today. That means you have free time until your five o'clock appointment. Oh; and this is a letter David left for you. It's marked personal, so I didn't open it."

She took the letter into her private office, and locked the door. She sat on her Louis the XIV sofa, and then opened the letter. She silently scanned the letter and smiled, which indicated some degree of pleasure. Then she read the letter out loud, to herself.

"Dear Dr. Crawford---Before you tear this letter up, please, please read it. I haven't been able to sleep at night, just thinking of you. I'm so confused. As you said, you took my case for nothing. You've helped me in so many ways. I keep asking myself why?"

She put the letter in her lap, as she asked herself, "Why David, indeed why?"

As she picked up the letter to reread it again, the phone signal flashed.

"Yes. Sharon," there was a pause. "Tell Susie to call back in an hour. Tell her I'm busy at the moment."

Time went by, and Dr. Crawford was in session with nervous, young Betty "what's her last name."

"I get frightened sometimes, Dr. Crawford. Would I really be able to hurt my own baby?"

Dr. Crawford took out her flashlight. "I am going to hypnotize you, so you will not be able to hurt your baby. Then we'll plan a course of treatment, to get to the root cause of your depression."

CHAPTER FOURTEEN

It was early evening now, and Susie was getting more agitated. She was still trying to reach Dr. Crawford. Tears were falling from her eyes.

"No Sharon, I do understand. Yes... No. I'm OK. I just want to talk to her. I understand she's got a patient. No I'll wait, or I'll just call back again."

There was a momentary pause. "Okay...she'll be in her office late, and I will be able to reach her. Okay I'll call back later." Sharon didn't recognize the level of desperation that Susie was portraying

Susie hung up the phone, and dialed her father's number. "No", she shouted, "no" as she heard, "You've reached the answering machine of Dr. Vargas. Please leave a message." The machine then added, "The message machine is full. Please call back later."

Susie hung up the phone, and continued to write the letter to her father.

Daddy, where are you? I can't get through to Dr. Crawford. I don't know what to do. I feel like a cloud is over me. I'm drowning, choking. I've got to speak to Dr. Crawford. I've got to.

Back in Dr. Crawford's office, Sharon was about to walk Betty out the door. David had arrived, and was sitting in the waiting room.

Dr. Crawford instructed Sharon to make an appointment for Betty for Monday at five o'clock. Then she told David to go into the therapy room, and to wait for her.

"And Sharon, you can go now. Please lock the security door downstairs on your way out. This neighborhood is starting to get seedy at night." Dr. Crawford then went over to the small file cabinet in her private office. She selected a file labeled Personal-For- My-Eyes-Only.

Sharon took her jacket, and left. Dr. Crawford waited for a moment, and then she locked the door. She turned off the ringer to the telephone, and lowered the volume of the answering machine. Then she returned to the therapy room. As she entered the room, her eyes and David's locked on each other. She walked over to where David was sitting, turned her chair to face him, and sat down.

Susie's desperation was building. She phoned Dr. Crawford's office again, and heard her message.

"This is Dr. Mary Crawford. I am unable to answer my telephone. Speak slowly, and leave your name and telephone number when you hear the beep."

"Please Dr. Crawford, its Susie. I need you. I can't help myself I can't go on anymore. I have to speak to you. Please...help me...I need you."

Susie hung up the phone, and waited impatiently for Dr. Crawford to return her unheard message.

CHAPTER FIFTEEN

"I read your letter, David."

"I hope you're not mad or upset."

"David, go into my private office, and wait for me on the sofa. I'll be right there."

Dr. Crawford stayed behind to readjust the furniture, as David walked into her private office. He had never been in this room, and as he looked around he saw a sweater draped over the chair in front of the roll top desk. He saw an answering machine with the red light blinking. He saw a sweater on the chair, and David quickly took it, and covered the answering machine. Then he sat on the small couch, as Dr. Crawford entered the room and sat next to him.

"David, I'm going to tell you a bit of my history. You'll learn a lot about me that no one knows. Not even Sharon."

Dr. Crawford opened the file. There were pictures and news articles. She held up one of the pictures.

"Here's a picture of a young man I met thirty years ago."

The resemblance to David was remarkable. "Wow, he looks a lot like me."

David moved close to her, so that they were touching. He put rested his arm on the back of the couch behind her. There was intimacy in the position.

"Yes, he did look a lot like you. And here is a picture of me, and a young man at my graduation from Berkley University."

A much younger Dr. Crawford was in a gown. The boy next to her was wearing a tuxedo. Together they made a handsome couple. "His name was Daniel. He was a twenty year old art student. You remind me very much of him."

Susie was dialing another number.

An operator answered, "Westwood General."

"Is Dr Crawford there?" There was a brief pause "I know her schedule says she's at her office. No, I don't want to talk with anyone else."

She hung up the phone, and continued to write to her father.

Daddy, I've got to go to her office. I know she's there. She's got to be there.

Dr. Crawford and David were continuing.

"David, there is some thing I want to tell you. Then we have to put these feelings to rest.

"David, I haven't been with anyone else since then. I know how wrong it is, but I haven't wanted anyone else, until you."

Susie walked out on the street. She was crying as she was walking. People noticed her, but she paid no attention to them.

She walked past Duke's restaurant, and soon arrived at the downstairs door of Dr. Crawford's office. She tried the door, and found that it was locked.

Confused and in a daze, Susie went to the telephone booth across from the office. She saw the lights on in the office, as she dialed the number.

"Please answer. You have to be up there. Please, please, please, in the name of God, please answer."

"What happened to him," David asked.

"We got married... My parents were furious. He was also much younger than I was. He left school, and we both got jobs. We made enough money, but his art suffered. He became depressed. I was so happy, that I never realized how bad he felt. Soon he started to use Heroin. Now I blame myself, but then I got so mad, that I kicked him out."

Dr. Crawford had tears coming from her eyes. When she regained her composure she continued.

"This is a brief article telling how he died the next day, overdosing and driving his car off a bridge."

David put his arms around her to comfort her. She turned her face to him, and they kissed. He realized he had crossed a line, and asked her if she was mad at him.

"No, I'm not mad or upset. Actually, I'm a little flattered. David, you're a very handsome young man. You could have any young girl."

"I don't want any young girl. I meant it when I said that I love you."

Across the street, Susie was holding the telephone, while looking up at the office window. She saw them kiss and continue to embrace. David slowly undressed Dr. Crawford, and he also took his own clothing off. Their foreplay was physical and passionate, as they proclaimed their love for each other. As Susie was watching she imagined David metamorphosing into the man who raped her. Dr. Crawford became Susie. In her mind, he was beating and chocking her. He was dragging her around with the leash and choker chain. In her mind, she heard her attacker telling her that she was his filthy bitch dog. 'I'm going to fuck you like a bitch dog', while his riding crop continued to raise welts on her body.

Somehow, she blindly stumbled home. She finished her letter.

"Daddy, she's fucking the boy. She's fucking me. Daddy, Dr. Crawford, Daddy, Daddy, I can't take it anymore."

David and Dr. Crawford were having sex. She turned, so that her back was to David. She was leaning over the back of the couch. When they finally finished, feeling totally drained, they slowly got dressed. Dr. Crawford saw that her answering machine was covered with her sweater. She removed the sweater, and saw that the machine was blinking.

"I guess I covered it."

"Wait a minute David; let me see who has been calling."

Dr. Crawford turned on the answering machine. Together they listened to the messages, as they got more and more frantic.

"Should we do something?"

"It will be all right, David. You run on home now. I'll wait for Susie's call."

When Susie didn't call back, she went home still thinking about David.

The next morning, Dr. Crawford was in her home having a cup of coffee. She put out an English muffin, some butter and jam. The sound system was playing some easy listening music. She was still in her pajamas, with a fluffy robe over them. She was the picture of domestic bliss, as she contemplated the possibility of a life with David. Why not? If it worked for him, it would work for her.

Her newspaper was folded over next to her coffee cup. Dr. Crawford lit up her first cigarette of the day, and then took her first sip of coffee, while she opened her newspaper. Suddenly she spit out her coffee. She dropped the newspaper, and gagged as she saw the picture of Susie smashed on the concrete.

"FAMOUS SURGIONS DAUGHTER JUMPS TO HER DEATH. Two hours of attempts by the L.A.P.D to talk her down fails."

Immediately Dr. Crawford called David.

"David look at today's newspaper. Don't say a word to anyone about last night. I'm going to take care of everything. Nobody can know you covered my answering machine. I'll explain everything to you when I see you."

Dr. Crawford was conflicted between her love for David, and her guilt. She rightly blamed herself for Susy's death. Her need to protect herself, and David was greater then her guilt. She rushed to her office, and erased all the telephone messages. She also shredded all of Sharon's notes.

CHAPTER SIXTEEN

I t was hours later that same morning. David was standing outside the upstairs door. He knocked three times, and then twice more.

"Who is it?" a voice called from the inside.

"B four," David answered.

As the door opened, there was a huge biker blocking David's way.

"Who the fuck are you?"

"I'm a friend of Karl's. He said it was cool."

Snap was walking by, and saw David. "He's OK, Fang. Come on in man."

David walked by the huge and menacing doorkeeper. There was a crack party going on, and the scene was similar to the one he saw earlier, except it was even wilder. There were twenty people in the room. The air was filled with loud music, and smoke from the base hits.

Snap had David by the arm, and he led him through the people and the furniture, to his usual corner of the room. His puppy was there, and it was very relaxed. The noise and the smoke didn't seem to bother him.

Snap boasted, "You've come on a good night. There's a party going on tonight. Of course you're not a member of the club, so you'll have to pay your way. Do you have any money?"

"I've got money. Plenty of money."

David was shaking, as he started to reach into his pocket.

Snap stopped him, and instead handed him a pipe.

"Do a hit first man; I sort of owe you one anyway. Are you OK?"

David looked at Snap in a very odd way. He hesitated then he told Snap, "I killed her, man…It was my fault that she jumped last night."

Then David lit a torch and took his first hit.

It was the afternoon of the same day. The group was at Duke's restaurant, without David.

Duke inquired if they had a good session.

Valarie answered, "We didn't have a session yet. Did you see the news in the paper? That girl, who jumped and killed herself, was a patient of Dr. Crawford."

"She never came here with you kids."

"She wasn't part of our group. She was a private patient. But we all feel like we knew her. We feel like she was a part of us. She was so young…and so pretty."

Valarie started to cry, as Peter put his arm around her to comfort her.

Karl asked Duke if he had seen David.

"No Karl, not today."

Duke saw a copy of the newspaper and picked it up.

"Let me see that a minute. I saw that girl last night. She was crying, and walking, maybe more like stumbling going north."

Later that day, the group was seated in its usual arrangement in the therapy room.

"We are all deeply saddened by the unfortunate death of Susan Vargas. We're going to spend some time today, to examine the effect it's had on each one of you."

Karl spoke up. "Dr. Crawford, do you know where David is? I'm kind of worried about him."

"I want each one of you to worry about yourself. While you are young, death seems very remote. When you are confronted by one of your peers, you have to face your own mortality. When you are in recovery, this is a particularly difficult time to face it. You are very vulnerable."

Peter brought up what Duke told them. "Maybe she was trying to come here."

Dr. Crawford answered sounding annoyed, "Stop it! Conjecture is of no value. We don't know everything, not even me, on what goes on in a diseased mind. I was here last night in a private session."

Karl chimed in, "With David."

"With David, yes," Dr. Crawford was angry. "But that girl didn't try to call me! Not even once."

Valarie joined in, "Nobody said that, Dr. Crawford. We're just worried about David. Maybe he saw the girl. Maybe they bumped into each other. We're just worried."

Dr. Crawford tried to deflect the group.

"David is a particularly sensitive young man. He is probably somewhere sorting out his own mortality. Let me worry about David."

Back at the crack house, the party was still going strong. It was night outside. Inside, David was sitting on the floor watching Snap do a big hit of base.

"Come on man! Just one! Give me one more hit. Then I won't bother you again. One hit for the road."

"David, do you know how many times you've said that? You've been smoking for eight hours now. You used up your three hundred dollars a long time ago."

"I gave you my watch too; I'm good for a hundred bucks credit."

"We don't give no credit here man. And you also smoked up your watch a long time ago."

Karl came in the door, as Snap was trying to tell David that he was done. Karl spotted David, and walked over to him.

"Karl, tell Snap that I'm good for it. Tell him to give me one more hit."

"David, what did I do to you? Come on, I'm getting you out of here."

"Please Karl, loan me ten dollars. Just let me do one more blast."

Karl took David by his arm, and led him out into the hallway. He was not angry, he was heartbroken, as he blamed himself for being the reason that David was there.

"It's my fault, I'm sorry David. We've got to dry you up."

Karl took David to his apartment. It was a neat studio apartment, with a small sofa, a chair, and a few end tables. There was a dresser in the corner, a Murphy bed, a television, and a stereo. There was a big blown up picture of a Harley Davidson, with a young Karl sitting on it. He was holding a first place trophy in one hand. There was also a young Terri Lane, looking like a prom queen, sitting on the back of the Harley.

David was sitting on the couch, shivering and sweating, as he "came down" from his high. Karl was sitting next to him.

"Karl, this is the worst part of it. I hate this part of it."

"It will pass soon. Keep remembering that. It will pass soon."

"I feel so bad, Karl. I let you down. I let the whole group down. I let Dr. Crawford down."

"You didn't let me down, or the group. You let yourself down man. Nobody, but yourself. Me and the rest of the group are here to pick you up. To help you be strong. That's how we all stay strong."

"I've let Dr. Crawford down though."

"No you haven't. Look, she's getting you so twisted, making you think you're falling in love with her. It's no wonder you relapsed. She should know better."

"Karl, no," David was getting hysterical now. "She's worked so hard to help me, and keep me straight. It's not her fault, Karl. None of it is her fault. And I do love her! That's just the way it is."

It was now evening, and Dr Crawford was leaving her office. She was leaving some last minute instructions with Sharon.

"Thank you for staying late, Sharon. I want you to cancel all my appointments for the next two days. Just reschedule them. There are a lot of extra details that I have to attend to, in the wake of the Vargas girl's death. I have to go to the Melville Art Gallery tomorrow. There is a showing that will directly benefit Westwood General Hospital's psychiatric medicine department. Please make sure that all my calls are diverted to the hospital, and that any emergencies are transferred to the doctor on duty tomorrow night. I don't want any other tragedies. Also try to call David's apartment until you reach him. Tell him that I must see him in the morning at my office. Then leave word on my private message line. Good night, Sharon."

CHAPTER SEVENTEEN

Meanwhile, that same night, Karl was with Terri at her apartment. Her apartment was very feminine, with one bedroom, a living room, and a kitchen. It was spotlessly clean and decorated with dainty touches. They were sitting on a couch, and the tone of their conversation was heated.

"Karl, you've been trying to find reasons to stop seeing Dr. Crawford right from the start! You never would make a clean break from your motorcycle gang. Now look what you've done."

"What I've done! What I've done!"

"What you've done Karl! Face it, and face any responsibility that is yours."

"Terri, I do face my responsibilities. But listen to what that woman did."

"How do you know that what David told you is true? How do you know that she actually seduced him? He wants to think that, and his mind is so confused right now."

"Terri, I'm not going back to her."

"Karl! David wanted her."

"Terri, I'm telling you, that woman is evil. I'm not going back."

"Then I don't want to ever see you again, Karl!"

The following morning David met Dr. Crawford in her office. There was no one else there so they sat close together.

"Dr. Crawford, I'm so sorry…" David wanted to express his regret for getting high, but Dr. Crawford misinterpreted him.

She reached over, and tenderly touched his cheek in a motherly way.

"David, it's all right. I think there's no way that anyone will find out about what happened when Susie killed herself. I've erased all the messages on my machine. The police are satisfied that it was a suicide. So there is nothing to indicate our responsibility. We have to not see each other, outside of the group for a while. If we are smart this will eventually pass."

It was now the evening. The rest of the day was spent with the good doctor tying up loose ends.

The Melville Art Gallery was rather small, and the exhibit was some of the worst art ever shown under one roof.

There was an equal mixture of men and women. They ranged in age from their early thirties, to their sixties.

The women were mostly attractive, and the men all looked wealthy. They were viewing the charity art exhibition

Hors d'oeurvres and wine were offered to the attendees.

Dr. Crawford was there dressed in a low cut, very beautiful and very expensive black gown. Three middle-aged men crowded around her, and she was talking and laughing in a charming way.

Suddenly, Dr. Vargas entered the room. He had left the convention in Las Vegas immediately, upon receiving the news of his daughter's death.

He was dressed in a black and grey tuxedo, and he looked extremely fit and suntanned. He had a smile on his face, as he walked over to Dr. Crawford.

Not knowing what to expect upon seeing his approach, she waited cautiously.

She was surprised as Dr. Vargas reached out, took her hand, and then kissed it in a European fashion.

"Dr. Crawford I expected you might be here, as this little affair is directly related to your fine department at Westwood General." Dr. Vargas led her away from the crowd.

"It's so nice to see you. I've wanted to call you, to express my deep regrets about Suzanne. She was so depressed. I thought I was getting through to her. She just gave me no indication that she was in eminent danger."

"My dear Dr. Crawford. Do you remember when I said to you that we are not gods? I didn't expect that you were a god, although I must say, you do look like a goddess."

Dr. Crawford smiled in appreciation of the compliment.

"I lose patients. I can't save all of them, in spite of my expertise and devotion. Nobody bats one hundred percent."

"Dr. Vargas, it's my job to bring comfort to you. You, my dear, are making it possible for me to accept the tragic loss of your lovely daughter. I do take each of my patients personally."

A well dressed, very thin man of sixty walked up, and vigorously shook Dr. Vargas's hand. "Dr. Vargas, so good to see you. I've read your entries in the medical journal. The work you are doing, discovering new meaning in the function of the thalamus, in how it affects the psycho chemical balance in the rest of the brain... fascinating!"

"Thank you, Dr. Pettrie."

"Good to see you out and about. It is the best medicine, when one suffers a loss. My condolences." Dr. Pettrie walked away.

Dr. Vargas took Dr. Crawford's hand. "He's right, you know. That's what I'm doing now. My work was always my life. Now it's even more so. I am discovering ways at isolating enzymes that control most of the autonomous reactions of response and stimulus. I've been working on synthesizing them. I have developed some enzymes that can be applied through the epidermis, in the form of a salve. These enzymes will be a vital tool in your therapy."

"That sounds fascinating Dr. Vargas. The implications are astounding."

They looked at some of the paintings, as their conversation continued.

"Mary, is it all right if I'm not so formal? I hope you don't mind me saying this, but did you know the art at this showing is awful?"

Laughing Dr. Crawford replied, "I was just thinking the same thing."

"You've done your duty here tonight. Please, help a grieving father. I have something I want to share with you. My own way of saying thank you my dear lady, for all you did for my Susan."

"What would you like me to do, Doctor?"

"I want to show you some of my research. I have my own personal laboratory, in the basement of my home. Come with me and let me show you some marvelous secrets. It will fascinate you."

"When?"

"Now."

"Now?"

"Yes now."

Dr. Crawford gave him her arm.

Dr. Vargas lived in a large, old house in Beverly Hills. There was a lot of distance between his house, and his neighbor's. She felt a sense of excitement as they pulled into his driveway. They entered the house into the foyer. There was a door that led to the basement. The rest of the house was dark. Dr. Vargas took her coat, and hung it in the closet.

"Allow me my dear. We are all alone. I've given my staff a few weeks off. I just wanted my work, and my solitude to help me to mend. But now with you...well, it helps."

They descended into the basement.

"Susan told me in therapy, that her mother, your wife, died in childbirth. You never remarried?"

"No, there was just my work, and my beautiful Susan. Now there's just my work."

The basement was a huge room finished with dark-paneled walls. Some of the room was lit. There was a stainless steel table, with a bright light over it. On the table were two dozen test tubes and other objects. They all contained different brain experiments in progress. Some were being boiled, some were slow heated, and some were frozen. There were partially dissected brains. They were labeled "Human," "Chimpanzee," "Canine," "Paranoia," "Fear," "Passion," and "Contentment."

The walls had posters showing many sexual predilections. Scenes depicted domination, bondage, humiliation, sadism, love, homosexuality, lesbianism, animalism, dismemberism, and cannibalism. The posters were all of good quality, and were very graphic.

There was a large refrigerator, with a large freezer, and two chairs. One was a bondage chair, with straps, stirrups, and other controls. The other was a hard stool. The walls that held the montage of posters were spotlighted. The bondage chair was in low light, so that the details of it were not evident.

Dr. Crawford first saw the table that held all the experiments. She was fascinated. Then her attention was drawn to the posters. As she started to examine them, Dr. Vargas drew her attention back to the table.

"This laboratory is the heart, and soul of all my experimental work on physic-chemical-psycho response. I have eight experiments in progress at this very moment."

Dr. Vargas pointed to the first test tube. "This contains fluids taken from the brain of a victim of a rape-murder. The kid choked the poor woman to death, while he copulated with her. Her brain sent impulses that were a mixture of fear, sexual stimulation, and sexual denial. Do we know yet what signals the brain sends off at that microsecond, when the brain accepts that death is inevitable? It's utterly fascinating, don't you agree, dear lady?"

"It is amazing, Dr. Vargas."

"Yes, of course it is. The brain is the most fascinating part of the living organism. We are just starting to understand a fraction of its workings. But of course you know that."

"But there is so much that you could teach me," she answered.

Dr. Vargas pointed to another experiment. "That is true, and I will teach you much. This is an example of a highly developed extract, taken from the brain of a man who was a serial killer. Now what makes this of particular interest to you, my dear, is that this man was under deep hypnotic analysis, when he suffered a heart attack and died. So you have a psychotic highly developed mind, which was under hypnotic influence when he died. The secretions brought about in such a mind, while under hypnosis are amazing. If we can isolate them, and synthesize them, you would have startling applications in your discipline of medicine."

"Is that possible?"

"More than possible. I have done it."

Dr. Crawford walked around the table with an air of reverence. Then she glanced at the posters on the walls. Dr. Vargas watched her, and then led her over to them.

"This, Dr. Crawford, is a gallery that has proved itself most valuable to me. So many of the aberrations of the brain, of the human spirit if you will, are controlled by our sexual impulses. Reproduction is perhaps the most important of our life functions. I have found sexual deviation, to be the primary stimuli for enzyme secretion. I strongly theorize that excessive secretion is the cause of much sexual aberration. Don't you agree?"

Dr. Crawford was so fascinated by all she was seeing, that she barely noticed how radical Dr. Vargas had become. He was acting out of control, and didn't wait for a response. He just continued on. "The Marquis De Sade. Oh how I would have loved to have his brain here. At any rate, I promised you that I would share a wonderful discovery with you."

Dr. Crawford started to become alarmed by Dr. Vargas's behavior.

"It's all quite fascinating. But it's getting late."

"No, buts Dr. Crawford! I am going to show you much, and teach you much."

Dr. Vargas took her roughly by the arm. She put up a little resistance. She felt threatened, and uncomfortable, but not in eminent danger. Dr. Vargas pulled her to the bondage chair.

"Sit in the chair, Dr. Crawford."

"No, I really think it's time for me to leave."

Dr. Vargas hit her in the head with his fist. She was stunned and groggy, as she fell into the chair.

Dr. Vargas strapped both of her hands, and feet with the restraints.

As Dr. Crawford regained her senses she was terrified. Dr. Vargas had gone over the edge, as he paced back and forth, raving at her.

"My good doctor, much of what I have learned, I will share with you."

He reached into his shirt pocket, and took out the letter that Susie had written to him.

"Just today, as an example, I found a letter that my daughter wrote to me. She started the letter the morning of the night she died. She wrote about the horrors of her ordeal. She wrote all day,

Doctor. She wrote how she called, and called, and called you. Each time she was getting more and more desperate. She wrote about the Doctor I trusted my daughter's sanity with. The Doctor; the women, whom she could trust. The only one who could have saved her? Yes she went to your office to see you, but she was locked out. She tried again to call you, but she saw that you were too busy fucking some young boy, and choking that boy. Driving my Susan over the edge, into insanity."

Dr. Crawford was crying and whimpering. "No, Dr. Vargas. There's a mistake here. A terrible mistake."

"LIAR," Dr. Vargas smacked her across her face, and then he backhanded her.

"You killed my Susan. You took her away from me. Do you see this work Doctor? It means nothing to me. My daughter was my life. You've destroyed her, and I will destroy you."

Dr. Vargas took a couple of deep breaths, as he tried to compose himself. Then he went about the rest of his actions, in a deliberate manor. "I will destroy you."

He took out a jar that held some strange looking cream. It was an off white color.

"I told you I would share my work with you. This cream has been developed for a secret military application. When I put some on you, you will become highly paranoid. You will be susceptible to hypnotic recall. You will remember the horror of being raped, beaten, and sodomized."

Dr. Vargas put a liberal quantity on her forehead.

Then Dr. Vargas pulled over an intravenous hookup, like one would find in a hospital. He put some cream into a bag of I.V. solution. Then he injected the solution into the vein in her left arm.

"Because, Doctor, that is what I'm going to do to you."

He then reached into a shadowy part of the room, and brought out some whips, and other instruments of torture, domination, and sexual abuse.

He raised the whip, and struck Dr. Crawford with the first of many blows as he fulfilled all his promises.

"I'm going to beat you, rape you, and burn you. I'm going to teach you, you filthy bitch. You are the worst bitch I've ever known."

The torture lasted for several hours. Finally, he drove Dr. Mary Crawford home and kicked her out of his car.

"Dr. Crawford, its David. I'm sorry to call you so late. I was getting worried about you. I've been calling you for hours." There was a pause. "Are you sure you're all right? I got Sharon's message."

"Listen David, don't come to my office. Come to my home. Come early when no one will see you."

It was early morning, and David was in her apartment. Dr. Crawford had black eyes, cuts, and abrasions. Her face was swollen, and she had black and blue marks on her arms. She was wearing a robe, so the whip marks on her body couldn't be seen. She was limping, and showing the effects of her ordeal at the hands of Dr. Vargas. David was visibly worried about her. He was also furious with Dr. Vargas. He was torn with guilt, grief, and love.

"That man is an animal. Look at what he did to you. Will you be all right? I ought to kill him. I ought to go over, and break his face. Are you sure you're all right?"

Dr. Crawford was moved by David's reaction. She reached over, and touched his cheek. "My darling David, my sweet, sweet David. I'll mend. I'll heel."

Dr. Crawford started to cry again, as the ordeal came back to her. She shook violently. David held her until the shaking stopped.

"Have you reported this? He'll go to jail you know. Have you called the police?"

"David, he has a letter that he says is from Susie. If I call the police, he says he'll give them the letter. He may give it to them, even if I don't call the police."

"What letter? What does it say?"

"Lies! Terrible lies about me. The letter would ruin me; I could even go to jail."

"You could deny it, whatever the letter says."

"Deny what a dead child has written? She's dead, David. I can't impeach her words. Even if I was believed, my career would be ruined."

"I'm not going to let him do this to you. It was my fault, not yours, mine."

David was starting to cry. His emotional state was ready to explode.

"No David, it was my fault. I shouldn't have let this happen. I'm your Doctor. It was wrong to love you."

"Love isn't wrong. Love can't be wrong."

David got still for a moment. Then he continued. "I'm going to kill him."

"No David!" Dr. Crawford put her hands on David's arm to restrain him. She was in obvious pain. David pulled free.

"It's the only way. He'll destroy you. He's an animal."

David was over the edge now. He was crying and raving. "I've got to kill him. I've got to."

CHAPTER EIGHTEEN

David was in his car driving aimlessly, and slightly erratically. He drove around the same block repeatedly.

He stepped on the brake to stop at an intersection; the car went into a skid, and hit a divider. He was not going fast, so there was no damage to the car, but David hit his head. He was not injured, but he was stunned. He pulled the car over to the curb where there was a pay telephone. His emotional condition was in shambles, and silent tears fell from his eyes as he dialed a telephone number.

"Please Karl, please answer. The phone was ringing, but there was no answer. David tried another number. His hands were shaking so badly, he had to try three times before he pushed the right buttons. Now he found himself stumbling over his words.

"Terri! This is David. Is Karl there? I'm in terrible trouble. I've got to talk to him."

"David, what's wrong? Where are you? No, you can't do that. Take a deep breath, and try to relax. Tell me what's wrong."

David sobbed as he related the entire story to Terri.

Meanwhile, the party at the clubhouse was still going strong. People were still smoking crack. Men and women were sitting all over. Some were sleeping in positions with arms and legs entwined half on or half off the mattresses. In one corner, there was a young girl shooting up heroin. Her biker boyfriend was watching her with a look of approval on his face. He had just finished shooting up himself.

Karl was standing near the chair, in his usual place, where we saw him before. Again he seemed apart from the rest of the par-tiers. Snap walked up toward him with a loaded pipe in his hands. He was showing the effects of the marathon crack party. His puppy was lying on the floor, in his usual place. Snap's voice showed the strain of smoking crack for so long.

"Hey, man. I've been partying non-stop for days now. You came up here last night, and you still haven't done a hit. Give it up man... Come on, get high!"

"I know man. I'm not sure what I'm doing yet. I'll start soon."

Terri was at Karl's apartment. She used the key Karl gave her so long ago, and let her-self in. The apartment was a little messier than it was before.

There was no answer when she called out to him. She then picked up the telephone, and called his work number.

"Hello, Mr. Donovan. This is Terri Lane, Karl Berber's girl-friend. Karl doesn't usually work on Saturday, but would you know if he was called in today?"

There was a pause, and then she learned that he had not been at work the day before either.

"Thank you. No, he's not in trouble. But a friend of his is."

Terri put the phone down, and talked to herself. "Where is he? I bet he's at that damn clubhouse."

Dr. Crawford was dressed. She had applied heavy make up to cover the bruises. She had sunglasses, so her black eyes didn't show. She went to her desk, and took a small revolver that she kept in a drawer, and put it in her purse.

"I've got to stop this, I've got to," she kept repeating.

Few people were walking in the street. The stores were all down-scale, most of them out of business, and closed. There was a pawn shop, a Goodwill store, a cheap clothing store, and a shoe repair shop. That's all that were left. Terri hurried by them all.

The scene was still much the same as before. The man and the girl last seen shooting up, were in a heroin induced stupor. Snap was sitting on the floor, talking to his puppy. There was a pipe, and a torch on a table next to Karl. He picked up the pipe, and lit the torch. Then Karl started talking to the pipe.

"All right you fucker. You won, or did I just lose, or did we both lose?"

Karl closed his eyes, and imagined how they were fifteen years ago. He saw a sign that said "Congratulations Star Quest Winners."

Under the sign, Terri and Karl stood side by side. There were cocktails, soda, and candy. A young man held out a mirror. On the mirror were lines of cocaine, and a rolled up hundred dollar bill. Terri said no, but Karl wanted to try one. Karl didn't know how it was done, so the young man showed him. Then, his reveries faded, changed, and he was in a clubhouse, much like the present one. Karl saw the first three bikers that he met. They told him to try something new, as they offered him a pipe. He remembered that he told them that he wouldn't, because his girlfriend was anti drug, in a big way.

"Come on; don't be a pussy. If you don't like the stuff then don't do it."

Karl took the pipe as the flashback ended. "If you were a man, I'd kill you. Now Terri doesn't want me, and I don't want you. But I guess you have me."

David started up his car again. He just slowly drove aimlessly in Hollywood, up and down Sunset Boulevard.

CHAPTER NINETEEN

While David was going nowhere, Dr. Crawford was driving her car. It was a bright sunny day, and her destination was very definite. The old house was magnificent in daylight. She got out of her Cadillac, walked directly to the front door, and rang the bell. She then opened her purse, and took out the gun. As she waited, she heard Dr Vargas inquire who rang. She threw her shoulder against the door with all her might. Not ready for this, Dr. Vargas was thrown backward. Dr. Crawford closed the door behind her, keeping the gun leveled at him, as Dr. Vargas regained his composure.

"Dr. Crawford, I presume. Did you like last night so much, that you had to come back for more?"

"I won't hesitate to use this gun if I have to, Doctor. Let's go down to your laboratory."

A police car was sitting at the corner of Sunset and Vine. There was one male and one female officer inside the car, who were engaged in idol conversation, while watching traffic.

The women officer behind the wheel was complaining about a comrade.

"You men can be such a pain in the ass. Pat is always bitching about duty. If he gets days, he wants nights. If he gets nights, he wants days. If he...;"

She stopped in midsentence. She noticed the almost robotic way that David was driving, as he ran a red light. "We better pull him over."

They pulled out of their parking space, and got behind David's car. They turned on their over-head lights, and followed him.

David saw the flashing lights in his rearview mirror, and ignored them while he continued his trance like driving.

Karl was still holding the crack pipe and the lit torch. He hadn't hit it yet. Suddenly, Terri was at the door, giving Fang the proper code to enter.

She was momentarily stunned when she saw Karl holding the pipe and torch. She rushed over to him.

"Oh Karl, I was wrong. I was so wrong about her, about Dr Crawford."

Karl put down the pipe and torch.

"Karl, David told me everything. Terri was sobbing, and almost hysterical.

"David is in terrible danger Karl. He's going to kill Susie's father. You've got to stop him."

Karl held Terri "Where is David now? What has she done to him?"

Karl gently shook Terri by the shoulders, to help her regain control.

Terri was still crying, as she looked around the room. "Why did you do this?" she said, gesturing to the pipe.

"Listen Terri; listen to what I have to say. I had to do this. I had to do it my way. I didn't do any crack, and I didn't shoot up. When you said that we were through, I believed you. I hated myself, but I had to do this for me. I had to come here, and not get high, even when I was hurting from losing you. For myself, do you understand? Even if I never saw you again, I had to prove something to myself. Maybe this was the wrong way, but it was my way."

"Karl, I love you. I would have come anyway. There is nothing without you."

"Terri, where is David?"

Snap walked over to them. He was still high, and a little drunk. He picked up the pipe, lit the torch, and held it toward Karl. "Come on man. Do your first hit."

Karl swung his hand at Snap's hand, and knocked the pipe to the ground.

"Fuck man. What the fuck? Why'd you do that?"

"Terri, let's get out of here."

David was still driving, oblivious to the police car behind him. He heard the police car's siren blip on and off, which got his attention. Then he heard the policeman announce over the speaker, "Pull your car over to the curb, and turn your engine off."

David's face contorted with anxiety. He took his gun out of the glove compartment, and put it on his lap "I won't pull over. I've got to kill him."

David pressed the accelerator, and sped up. He was weaving in and out of traffic, as he tried to lose the police car.

"Holy shit we've got a chase. I'll call it in."

The female officer accelerated in pursuit.

"This is car four twenty. We are in pursuit of a red Chevrolet, license number zebra- zero- two- four- Albert- one. We are west on Sunset Boulevard, going towards Beverly Hills. Driver has a gun that we spotted, and could be dangerous. Request assistance in pursuit. He might be heading for a freeway. Alert other agencies."

Dr. Crawford and Dr. Vargas faced each other. She held her gun pointing at Dr. Vargas. The room was as it was before. Dr. Crawford stood close to the experiment table. Her attention was drawn to the human brain. It was labeled Human Fear. It was held in a clamp that pinched it. There were wires attached to it that ran to attachments on the table. One was labeled "Electricity." A short tube had been inserted into the base of the brain, and through it dripped one drop of fluid into a shallow collector dish.

Dr. Vargas was not frightened. He was clearly a mad man.

"Now what my dear? Are you going to shoot me? Go ahead! Although I thought you'd be more clever than that. The police will tie you to my murder. They will find a connection. Instead of a second-degree murder charge for my daughter, it will be first-degree for my murder. I'm disappointed in you my dear."

Dr. Crawford doesn't answer him. She is momentarily mesmerized by the brain experiment.

Dr Vargas moved slightly towards her.

Dr Crawford, seeing him move snapped out of it.

"Don't! Don't move. I didn't come here to kill you; I came here to save you. One of my patients, a young boy, is coming here to kill you."

She then snatched Susie's letter, which was on the bench from the night before.

"But maybe I'll let him kill you. We'll make up an acceptable excuse. After all, you are a very sick man Doctor."

She then ripped Susie's letter into small pieces.

"And what if it doesn't work? What if he doesn't come? Or what if you fall under my spell again? Oh yes, it could happen. Those were very strong potions that I used on you."

Dr. Vargas's eyes had been boring into Dr. Crawford's.

"You'd be best to kill me now, and go to jail. Or just leave. Or perhaps my dear, you'd like to sit down in my chair."

Dr. Vargas slowly rotated the chair back and forth in a continuous motion. "Or should I say, in your domination chair in your chair, in your chair?"

Dr. Crawford was starting to go under. She shook her head to clear her mind.

"No, Dr. Vargas. I can fight you. I am stronger than you realize."

Dr. Crawford pulled out her flashlight, and turned it on. She centered on the flashlight, whenever she started to weaken. It was a battle of hypnotic wills.

David's car was speeding, and swerving around other cars. There were five police cars, and a helicopter in the pursuit. Other cars drove out of the way, but there had been four accidents, as a result of this segment of the chase.

Karl and Terri had just left the crack house, and were hurrying towards Karl's motorcycle.

"What is the address that David said?"

"Forty- two- hundred Rockefeller- Place, in Beverly Hills."

There was a noise, like a small explosion, from the loft crack house. They both looked towards the window, which shattered out onto the street below.

"Karl, my God. The loft's on fire!"

Terri and Karl stopped and watched, as the fire started to become visible from the street. The front door burst open, as bikers and women in various degrees of undress spilled into the street. Karl spotted Fang, and went over to him.

"How many were in the loft?"

"Twenty-two not counting you, and your old lady."

Karl started to look around and count. Suddenly the biker and his young girlfriend who were shooting heroin, leisurely walked out the door. Karl rushed up to them. Their eyes were all glazed. The biker looked at Karl.

"You two make twenty-two." The biker has no idea as to what Karl was talking about. "Wow what a bum trip."

David was now on the freeway. He was being followed as before. A few freeway accidents happened, as the chase continued.

Dr. Vargas was slightly closer to Dr. Crawford. They were still in a hypnotic stare down.

"And what if the hypnotic cream retakes command of you, my dear? Why not just submit to me? Be my slave my dear."

"I hope you feel great pain, when David shoots you. I hope you don't die too quickly."

The chair and flashlight dual continued.

The fire in the crack house was getting more intense. The fire department had just arrived; they surveyed the scene, and decided to let it be a burn down. Karl spotted Snap, and he and Terri ran over to him.

"Where's the puppy, Snap?"

"Fuck him man! He's still up there. We better all get out of here, before the "Pigs" get here!"

"I've got to save him." Karl rushed by Terri and Snap, into the burning building.

Terri cried, "No Karl," but she was too late.

The chase continued; with David's car now back on Sunset Boulevard. He was getting closer to Dr. Vargas's house.

Most of the bikers had now fled the scene. Some were too stoned to move.

Terri was waiting by the front door, watching it fearfully. It had been too long by now. How could this be happening? Then a smoke stained Karl, stumbled through the door. He was holding a shivering German shepherd puppy. Karl was dirty, and singed, but unharmed. He handed the terrified puppy to Terri. "Take care of the poor thing Terri. I've got to go and help David."

Terri put her hand on Karl's shoulder. "Please be careful, and come back to me my darling."

Karl roared away on his bike. A second police car pulled up at the fire scene, as the first policeman walked over to Terri.

David, the police cars, and now a helicopter sped past a sign that announced, "Entering Beverly Hills." David maintained a half block lead on the police.

The two doctors continued their deadly duel of hypnotic power. Dr. Vargas was slightly closer to Dr. Crawford.

CHAPTER TWENTY

"Please be careful, and come back to me, my darling. Please be careful and come back to me, my darling." Karl repeated to himself. She said it and she meant it.

Karl pulled up to Dr. Vargas's house. He got off his bike and went to the front door. He paused, and decided to look for a basement window through which to enter. He went to the back of the house.

In the basement, Dr. Vargas had inched up a little closer to Dr. Crawford. He was starting to win the battle of hypnotic wills. "It's too late, my dear. You can't resist me. I will put you back in your chair. In your chair. In your chair."

Dr Crawford still held the gun. She was mentally fighting for her survival.

Dr. Vargas had an expression of pure evil delight. He eased still closer toward to Dr. Crawford.

David pulled up to the "Vargas" house. He still had a half block lead on the police. The helicopter was still overhead. He got out of the car with the gun in his hand and walked slowly to the front door.

The helicopter called out through its public address system, "Drop the gun, and lie down on the ground with your hands behind your head."

Karl had found a window. He picked up a brick, and raised it to smash the window.

Dr. Vargas moved toward the gun that Dr. Crawford was holding.

The five police cars that had been following David pulled up and police piled out of the cars. One police officer shouted, "He's got a gun."

David ignored them. He was still in a trance.

Dr. Vargas's hand reached for the gun. Dr. Crawford had entered a light trance.

Karl smashed the window. He climbed through it, and was on a stairway leading to the basement door. He heard sounds coming from behind the door... He rushed to open the door where the two Doctors were.

Karl opened the door sharply, breaking Dr. Crawford's trance.
He saw the two doctors struggling for control of the gun.

The police fired a Teaser dart into David's back. He fell to the ground, and the gun dropped from his hand. Then the police rushed to handcuff him.

Dr. Vargas and Dr. Crawford were locked in combat for the gun. The gun exploded twice. Dr. Vargas had the upper hand, and Dr.

Crawford had been shot twice. She was shot once in the chest, and once in her face. She fell away dead.

At the front of the house, the police now had David in custody. They hoisted him to his feet, handcuffed him, and sat him on the curb. David put up no resistance, and sat submissively. "This guy is stoned, or something."

Then they heard the two shots from the house. "What the hell was that?"

The officer in custody of David told the others to check it out. Two officers drew their guns, and entered the house.

It was determined that David no longer posed a threat.

Dr. Vargas still held the gun. He was confused, and dazed, as he backed away from the dead woman.

Karl reached over to Dr. Crawford, and felt for a pulse in her neck. He found none. Her flashlight was shinning into her dead eyes.

"She's dead! You've killed her man."

Dr. Vargas was acting as if he was still in shock. He held the gun, pointing it at Karl, and Dr. Crawford.

The two police officers hurried down the stairs with their guns drawn.

They burst into the room, and quickly surveyed the scene.

"Put that gun down, and don't move anybody."

Dr. Vargas, still in shock, brought the gun up and pointed it at the police.

The police opened fire, and pumped twelve rounds into him.

Outside the county coroner's office van pulled up along with an ambulance to transport David to the hospital. His handcuffs were repositioned so his arms were no longer in back of him. He was sitting on the curb submissively, as he was been judged not to be a threat.

He saw Dr. Crawford's body being carried out of the house. The sheet that was covering her caught on the door. Her face was exposed. David saw it, and lunged at the nearest officer throwing him off balance, and grabbed his gun. He started to run towards Dr. Crawford while he held the gun before him, screaming. "She needs me. She needs me."

David was cut down by a hail of bullets. The shooting was over in five seconds.

Karl went over to David and dropped on his knees to hold him. David was bleeding onto Karl.

"No oh, no! He's just a kid. He didn't want to hurt anyone."

Terri had come over to Karl, and she was also crying. She put her arms around Karl.

"Why David, Terri, oh please God why David? Take me out of here. Please, Terri."

Terri got down with Karl, as he laid David down. She held Karl in her arms, and rocked him, and cradled his head to her breast to comfort him.

A Detective walked up to Terri and Karl, accompanied by the officer who drove Terri to the scene.

"Everything you've told Officer Kline here corresponds to what we've been able to piece together. You can go now Mr. Berber. We will have to talk to you some more about some details here, and about the fire. Stay clean, and come to my office tomorrow."

The detective handed Karl his business card.

CHAPTER TWENTY-ONE

Two nights after the carnage, the group is sitting at their usual table at Duke's. They are joined by Valerie's mother, Peter's father, and Andrew's parents. Terri is also there. The dress is casual, except for Valerie's mother, who is dressed in striking pants and blouse. There is food, ice cream sundaes, and soda in front of every one. No one is eating though.

The parents are sitting at one end of the table. They're chatting quietly.

The rest of the group is sitting kind of shell shocked. Peggy is crying, and Andrew is trying to comfort her. Her parents aren't there.

Peter's father announces, "Karl, we are all very grateful to you. The group, you know that's what we think of you all, the group has gone through hell. I am looking into another therapist, who will take you all. Sort of as a group."

"We're scared" Karl answered. "I'm talking for everyone. Right gang?"

"Can I say something?" Terri looked to Karl for approval and got it.

"You can't stop now. You're vulnerable all of you. Even you, Karl. You can't stop."

Valarie asks, "How can we trust anyone again? I'm so confused."

Andrew chimed in "I'm not going to any shrink again. Look at David. Look at all of us. It's not right!"

Andrews's father puts his foot down. "Andrew I'm afraid you'll do whatever we decide is best."

Duke was walking near the group, and discreetly listened. "Hey kids how are you holding up?"

"Not so good Duke."

Duke doesn't wait for an invitation. He pulls over a chair, and sits down. He's rewarded by Valarie's mother, with a dazzling smile.

"Listen. It's none of my business, but I've gotten to know you kids over the past few months. Even you grown ups have become, well friends."

The group nodded, but Peter's father interrupts. "This is all pretty serious business, Duke, and it's really private."

Peter and Valarie jumps to Duke's defense. "Wait! Duke's our friend."

"With all due respect," Duke intoned, "I probably know a lot more about them, that you realize. I get all kinds of customers in here. Some are not good at heart. These are all good kids, with problems. The overriding problem is addiction. Get that under control, and the rest of the problems will go away. Have you ever considered a twelve step program?"

Valarie's mother speaks up. "That's for drunks, and bums. My children need private care."

"That's kind of funny, because that's where I go."

"You, Duke?" Karl asks.

"I was strung out, messed up, and in bad shape. I've been clean now for ten years and I did it, one day at a time. All I'm saying is, if you really give it a try it works. It sure has for me."

It was a lovely spring day. The lovely old church was in a peaceful setting, overlooking the Pacific Ocean. There \were a lot of motorcycles parked, in front of the church. A sign announced the marriage of Terri Lane and Karl Berber.

Karl, now clean cut, was handsome in his tuxedo. Terri was radiant, wearing her wedding gown.

Terrie's parents were behind her. Peter's father and Valarie's mother were behind Karl, taking the role of his parents.

Andrew, Peggy, Valarie, Jeffery and Peter, were all there. They were all happy for Karl, but their hearts hung heavy for David. All members of the group looked happy, and healthy.

There were a lot of Karl's old motorcycle gang present. Some had cleaned up. Some hadn't. Snap couldn't come, since he's in prison.

Duke was there, and was Karl's Best Man. Valarie was beautiful as the Maid Of Honor.

The Minister began the ceremony.

"Friends it is an axiom that every journey begins with a first step. These two young people before me began their journey together five years ago. The course they choose to take has been very hard. But now with the grace of God, they will travel on together in wedded bliss.

I now pronounce you Karl Berber, and Terri Lane, Husband and Wife.

Terri and Karl kiss, as the whole church roared its approval. The couple hurried outside, and the whole group followed. There was a sign on the back of Karl's bike that proclaimed, "Just Married." Terri got on the bike after Karl. She tossed her bouquet, and Valerie caught it. A young boy handed the German shepherd puppy to Terri, and the newlyweds roar off.

The End

Flowers bloom, and their springtime promise is one of beauty. Life sometimes intrudes on nature's plan, and flowers become broken. Some can be mended, and some wither, and die.

AFTERWORD

The drug and alcohol crisis in this country is catastrophic. Hundred of thousands of lives are ruined. Thousands of lives are lost.

Billions of dollars are expended, between the purchase of addictive drugs, rehabilitation efforts, and incarceration. The money helps fund organized crime, and terrorism.

Parents, to quote Crosby, stills, Nash and Young; "Teach your children well, their father's hell did slowly go by."

We are first adult generation of the drug pandemic.

Who among us doesn't know someone that's been infected by it.

Preach to your children. Watch for signs. Be paranoid. Forget the politically correct concept of juvenile privacy. You had that child!

Bring him to adulthood safely!